# If the SHOE FITS

*Once Upon a Romance*
Book 1

# LAURIE LECLAIR

## DEDICATION

To the late Clifford W. Smith. Thanks, Dad, for teaching me how to dream.

To my husband, Jim LeClair, thank you for holding my hand and my heart for the last thirty-three years. Dreams do come true.

# CHAPTER 1

"Hey, lady, what's your rush? You gonna turn into a pumpkin or somethin'?" the taxicab driver asked as he tucked the fare and tip in his top pocket.

Charlotte King chuckled as she slammed the car door shut. She dashed through the drenching rain.

With one finger curled tightly around the metal garment bag hook, Charlie jumped into several puddles. She rushed up the walkway and stairs to the massive oak door guarding the stony fortress she once called home.

Under the shelter of the overhang, she caught her breath in the chilly night air. With her free hand, she brushed back the wet tendrils of dark hair from her cheeks. Cool droplets of rain slithered down the back of her neck, making her shiver.

In spite of her soggy condition, a smile tugged at the corner of her mouth at the evening ahead. The mandatory attendance tonight seemed a small price to pay if it could somehow assist in getting one of her stepsisters married. "One down and one to go," she whispered hopefully.

Her stepmother's offer this morning was too good to refuse. Charlie would use her many marketing talents and people skills to promote her stepsisters to their prospective grooms. In exchange, her stepmother promised invigorating new interest in the family store.

The implication lay there, thick and heavy, between them. King's Department Store, her late father's beloved store, would benefit immensely in the end.

And the store needed it more than ever. Charlie's heart had sunk after seeing the latest slumping quarterly sales reports in the managers' meeting earlier in the day. The grim news hit especially hard; the store couldn't keep this downward pace without someone suffering. Her stepmother had made it quite clear that layoffs were a foregone conclusion. How could they even think of getting rid of the faithful employees who had stuck with them for decades? They were like family to Charlie.

And, next on the chopping block would be the store itself. The holidays were just a few short months away. This season would make or break King's. She swallowed hard. It was do or die.

Charlie shook her head, clearing her mind of the dark outcome. She had to fix this. So many people were counting on her. She couldn't let them down. She had to perform to her stepmother's liking tonight and get the woman, who was in charge of King's and who controlled the purse strings, to release her stronghold on the store's remodeling and marketing budgets. In her heart of hearts, Charlie knew it would take drastic revamping to lure customers back in the declining store. But she could do it. She would save her father's store.

Visions of customers clamoring for their newest and finest goods and sales skyrocketing made Charlie giddy with anticipation.

In her bag she'd neatly tucked her sketchbook, pages filled with new layouts and future innovations to present to her stepmother in a private meeting after dinner this evening. Now, Charlie clutched it a little bit tighter; this could be the new beginning for King's.

All her father's dreams could come true. It was up to Charlie to make sure that happened. She'd promised him. It was a nine-year-old girl's promise to her dying father.

A promise was a promise.

And she'd lived that desperate need to honor him for nearly twenty years now, lived and breathed the store and his dream.

"Now this," she said softly. A part of it nagged at her. A marriage of convenience? Her stepsisters? Her parents had one, though. It had worked. They'd fallen deeply in love and were devoted to each other until the day her mother had died.

Love in a marriage of convenience could still happen, couldn't it?

"If only I could get the stepmother married off, too."
A shudder went through her, at the cool breeze rushing
over her damp body or the image of a man actually
brave enough to marry her stepmother; Charlie couldn't
be sure which thought had caused that particular
sensation.

She gave one last lingering look at her father's
house.

Yellow beams of light beckoned from the windows.
The fortress, awash in warmth and cheer, appeared
welcoming to all who needed refuge from this dark,
rainy night. It hadn't felt like her home since her father
died. A pang of nostalgia rushed through her.

Charlotte cast that sad thought aside and focused on
what lie ahead. Desperate times called for desperate
measures. She'd live up to her part. Once the distraction
of getting her eldest stepsister engaged was over, then
all Charlie had to do was convince her stepmother that
King's Department Store, the once grand family
business started by her late father, was worth saving
even in these hard times.

"One good deed deserves another, right?"

Smiling, she knocked on the hard wood. Her cold
knuckles ached at the rough contact. In the next instant,
the huge door flew open.

"Dolly," she cried, stepping into the foyer and
dropping the heavy black bag. She hugged the short,
round older woman who'd practically raised her. Curly,
gray hair brushed her cheek as she embraced her friend

and confidante. The hint of rose perfume and pressed face powder tickled her senses.

"Why, Miss Charlie, where have you been?" Dolly asked, pulling slightly away and holding her at arm's length. "And dripping wet, too." With a frown gathering between her usually sparkling blue eyes and shaking her head, she said, "You'll catch your death like that."

At the concern-laced chastisement, Charlie smiled widely, feeling loved. She shrugged. "I was being held hostage in a taxicab, of all places. When I got within a block, I hopped out and escaped down the street."

Dolly chuckled. Closing the door, she bent to pick up the dropped bag. "Oh, you're late. We'd better hurry up and get you changed. Did you bring the one I told you to?"

"Your favorite, just like you asked."

"And the shoes?"

"The shoes, too."

"That's my Charlie."

She nodded her head to the closed door of the formal living room. "Is the barracuda fuming?"

"Shush now, she'll hear you."

Charlie grinned. She'd been calling her stepmother Barracuda since the day her father brought his new bride home. The name couldn't have been more perfect for the razor-sharp tongued woman who zeroed in on her foe with lethal precision and attacked. Charlie had seen it a thousand times, both in her personal and professional dealings with the woman.

An impish delight took hold as Charlie asked, "And has Prince Charming arrived?"

"He has. Been waiting on you for half an hour, too."

"It's not me he's come to inspect for a bride."

The older woman tucked her arm through the crook of Charlie's elbow and steered her to the wide, elegant oak staircase. "If you ask me, them two stepsisters of yours in there can't measure up to the dimple on your backside."

"Why, Dolly, you've been looking again."

That had her friend giggling like a schoolgirl. Charlie joined in as they raced up the stairs to the guest bedroom. On the way, Dolly gossiped shamelessly, "My, he is a fine looking one, though-"

\*\*\*

Prince Charming, as the papers dubbed him, leaned his hand on the oak mantel above the fireplace, his back to the opulent gold parlor. Never in Alexander Royale's life had he wished to burst out laughing as much as he did now. He'd overheard the feisty exchange between the maid and the last sister in the outer foyer.

Barracuda? How perfect to describe the older, stern-faced woman behind him. If it hadn't been for her ongoing insistence, he'd have easily brushed off his grandfather's suggestion of dinner with the all-female King family.

But marriage was the goal, wasn't it? So here he was, searching for a wife to please his ailing grandparents. First the wedding and then the heir.

Under control, Alex straightened and slowly turned to the three seated women. He had to bite his inner cheek when he witnessed the same sour expression on all their faces. They'd heard.

Mrs. King, dressed in black from head to toe, smiled weakly at him. "More sherry, Mr. Royale? Francine will be happy to pour."

The girl in question, blonde with blue eyes, perched on the edge of the sofa with one hand clasped lightly over the other in her lap. One corner of her mouth shifted upward as she pasted on a smile.

"No, thank you, Mrs. King, Francine." The girl actually breathed a sigh of relief, which made Alex's lips twitch. He darted a glance in the other girl's direction.

Seated beside her sister, she could have been her twin in dress alone. Matching knee-length, plain black dresses with long sleeves adorned their waif-thin bodies. However, the other one, Priscilla he recalled, had her strawberry blonde hair swept up and her green eyes lowered.

By all accounts, Alex figured the mother was trying to marry off the oldest sister. Neither one appealed to him in the slightest. In fact, this whole business of plucking a bride out of a lineup made him ill.

He longed for the evening to end. Glancing at the gold-faced mahogany grandfather clock across the room, he nearly groaned out loud. It would be hours before he could make *his* escape, he thought as he recalled the overheard conversation in the foyer a short while ago.

It seemed like long, drawn-out hours of stony silence peppered with polite acceptable society inquiries. In reality, thankfully for Alex, it was only twenty minutes before he heard the maid outside the parlor door.

"Now, honey, you go and be yourself." Her cautionary tone held an unmistakable caring beneath it.

"I intend to."

"No need to kowtow to Her Highness or her little entourage. They ain't no better than you, you know? Never have been, never will be."

The light feminine chuckle that followed left a warm trail in his chest. Alex stood, to prepare for the last sister's entrance or to shake off that sensation - he couldn't be too certain. Either way, he wanted the night to end.

The door clicked open. He found himself holding his breath.

"Shoot," the younger voice cried. "My shoes-"

He caught a glimpse of the maid's profile, waving a hand at the woman still out of his sight. "Scoot back up there and get them. I'll hold the fort down by getting them to the dining room."

\*\*\*

Entering the elegant emerald green dining room, Alex calculated the number of hours remaining. He groaned inwardly at the stilted, forced conversation to come. He reminded himself he'd done this a hundred times before and he could do this again. But his jaw ached with the effort to keep a pleasant smile on his face.

"Ladies," he began, ready to extol on the gleaming silver, sparkling Waterford crystal, gold-edged plates, and the overflowing flower centerpiece. He stopped short when he heard what he assumed was the footsteps of the last sister racing down the stairs.

Alex turned just in time to see a whirlwind of red slide across the marble floor. The force hit him square in the chest.

# CHAPTER 2

He let out a soft grunt.

Instinctively, he reached out to hold her, protect her much smaller body. But she pulled away, taking away the warmth he'd experienced. A tantalizing scent lingered.

Brushing the rich chestnut, shoulder-length hair out of her eyes, she met his surprised gaze. "Oops!"

He smiled at her, holding back a bubble of laughter. If possible, her caramel-colored eyes twinkled and her lips stretched even more.

Behind him, Mrs. King scolded her, "Really, Charlotte! Must you always make a scene?"

It wasn't really a question. Charlie winked at him. "Of course, Stepmother, how else can I have any fun?"

"Charlotte King-"

"Yes, ma'am." She seemed to answer automatically like replaying a preprogrammed response used many times in the past. Her smile never faded and the mischievous way she rolled her eyes had Alex suppressing another chuckle.

Charlie held out her hand to him. "Why, if it isn't Prince Charming."

That was the last thing Alex expected her to say.

Stunned for only a moment, he chuckled. He grasped her hand. He swore he heard a quick intake of breath from her at the contact. Soft, smooth skin with perfectly applied red nail polish, he noted. The touch sent a flood of warmth from his palm through his body. He never wanted to let go. "You, my lady, are the only one to dare say that to my face."

He noted the red wrap dress hugging her curves and a glimpse of her long legs peeking through the mid-thigh slit. Then he realized she was in stockinged feet. She held a pair of strappy red high heels in her other hand.

"Charlie, is it?" He nodded to her shoes, asking, "May I help you with those?"

She giggled. As Charlie slipped on the left shoe, and then did the same to the right one, she said, "No thanks, I can do it myself, Prince Charming."

"Well, if the shoe fits," he teased her.

"Very clever. But that's only if a girl wants to be a Cinderella."

He laughed heartily. Charlie had clearly told him in no uncertain terms that she didn't need a prince, much less a man, to rescue her from anything. A spark of admiration lit in him.

She was the first woman in years who didn't see him as a great catch. How refreshing.

Mrs. King cleared her throat in obvious disapproval.

Turning to her family, Charlie nodded politely. "Stepmother, sisters."

Reluctantly, he followed suit. He encountered the flash of anger directed her way.

"Charlotte, you are late." Her stepmother's pinched mouth barely moved. "Poor Francine and Priscilla have been entertaining our guest while you were lollygagging."

"I'm sure they enjoyed every minute of having Mr. Royale to themselves, isn't that right, girls?" She brushed the accusation away with what seemed like practiced ease.

In turn, each girl's cheeks pinkened, making Alex think they looked much better now with some color.

Another throat sound came out. Another reprimand, Alex sensed. He turned back to help Charlie be seated. She'd already moved to her place on the other side of the table from him.

A stab of disappointment slashed through him. Surprised at it, he shook it off quickly, reminding himself how much he wanted to get this night over with.

"She was with Dexter again," Priscilla whispered loudly, uttering her first full sentence since Alex had arrived.

"Dex," Charlie corrected as she lifted her chin higher in defiance, but didn't deny the accusation.

His chest tightened. Who was Dex? Remembering his manners, Alex assisted Francine, who'd been assigned a seat beside his.

"Thank you," she murmured so softly that he'd thought it was just above a child's whisper.

He groaned inwardly, thinking this was the one they were trying to marry off to him. It was going to be a long night.

\*\*\*

From across the table, Charlotte watched in approval. He was a gentleman, though society tutored, but nonetheless a mannered one. That would be something the Barracuda and Francine would appreciate. Score one for Alexander Royale, she thought.

He was a handsome devil though, better than any of the papers had ever been able to capture. Dark hair, dark eyes, tall, and muscular: she recalled the broad, solid chest she'd bumped into and the strong arms that instantly had wrapped around her. Heat, a sexy musky scent...and his hand, strong yet gentle...

She brushed her fingers against her palm, still tingling from his touch.

Her lips parted at the memory of being in his arms. A rush of warmth coursed through her body. She'd never been so affected by a man in her entire life, never mind one she'd just met and in less than ten seconds.

Reluctantly, she pulled herself out of her reverie. She had a mission to accomplish: Get Francine married, and then she could save King's Department Store. She owed it to her late father to bring back his beloved store from the brink of demise.

Update and renovate, she'd often remind her stepmother when plunging sales reports littered Charlie's desk at work. The store, and how to restore it to its former glory days, consumed her more and more these days.

But now, gazing into Alexander Royale's laughing dark eyes, she felt a genuine pang of regret. What would it feel like to be in love just once?

Love and marriage weren't in the cards for her, she reminded herself, not now when she could do so much for King's Department Store. Maybe never. The store would always come first. She sighed heavily.

An hour later, she'd run out of things to champion her stepsister's cause. Charlie desperately searched for something, anything else to point out to him. "Oh, I almost forgot. How silly of me. Francine takes piano lessons. I'm sure you'd love to play something for Mr. Royale after dinner, Francie, wouldn't you?"

She noted how Alex quickly covered his mouth with his starched white napkin. To hide a smile or stump down a groan, she wondered mischievously. His narrowed, dark brown eyes met hers and she knew.

She was going to get hers. A shiver raced down her spine.

Halfway through the meal, Charlie's heart warmed even more at all the praise Alex heaped on her friend.

"This is delicious, Dolly," he complimented her for the fourth or fifth time. "Where in the world did you learn to cook like this?"

The cook, standing beside him, nudged his shoulder with her hand. "Aw, shucks, Mr. R. You keep sweet-talking me and I just may have to move in with you."

"Be my guest. In fact, if you ever want a change, I'll hire you and for twice as much as what the Kings are paying you."

Mrs. King let out an exasperated breath. "Oh, please. She's just doing what she's being paid to do. Cook, clean..." She waved a hand to encompass the house.

"Kowtow," Charlie interrupted.

The sisters gasped in unison. Her stepmother snapped her head around to stare directly at Charlie. The lethal, narrow-eyed gaze would have cut some men in two.

Charlie steeled herself, raising her eyebrows and said, "It's true."

Turning away, she caught Alex's gleaming stare and a ghost of a smile. This time, he was the one to wink at her. Another rush of warmth raced through her.

What was he doing to her?

\*\*\*

Charlie hated the drawing room or, at least, what the barracuda had done to it soon after her father had died. The now flowery, feminine room seemed far removed from the masculine room with rich, leather chairs, dark wood, and scent of cherry pipe tobacco that her father had favored. An ache of sorrow shot through her every time she entered this room and thought of the man she mourned for.

The sooner she could make her escape from here and go to the kitchen to be with Dolly the better for her, she thought, flinching at the sour notes Francine began to play.

\*\*\*

Alex plotted the throttling of Charlie for suggesting this as he endured yet one more painful tune from Francine. He winced as she missed another note, but quickly pasted a smile on his face as Mrs. King looked his way.

Thinking of Charlie had him searching the room in earnest. The little devil snuck out!

\*\*\*

Sitting across the table from her longtime friend, Charlie slid the spoonful of homemade cherry vanilla ice cream into her mouth. She moaned. "Heavenly."

Dolly pointed her spoon at another container between them. "Try the chocolate one. I betcha it's even better."

"I doubt that."

"Five bucks says I'm right."

"Nobody bets against a sure thing, Dolly," she said, knowing that her friend's claims were most likely true. But she did take a dip and taste. Closing her eyes, she savored every drop.

"See, I told you. Now pay up."

Charlie chuckled, opening her eyes once again. "You're a dream, my friend. You could make a fortune going into business with just your ice cream alone, never mind all your other concoctions."

She noted the pink coloring Dolly's cheeks. "Aw, shucks, honey."

"At least you got a job offer from the prince." She raised and lowered her brows a few times. "That could be mighty interesting."

"You're telling me! My, that man is gorgeous. And the way he looks at you—"

"No he doesn't," she interrupted quickly, her throat going dry.

"Yes, he does."

"No—"She stopped herself short. The memory of his dark eyes on hers, his sexy smile, muscled arms wrapped around her… Her cheeks warmed. "Maybe," she said softly.

Dolly snorted, but didn't say another word.

The high, tinny notes from the piano reached Charlie's conscious now. "It doesn't matter. He's Francine's anyway."

"If you say so," Dolly said sourly, lifting an eyebrow as she stared meaningfully at her.

"He is."

They both cringed at the next resounding note and heard the sisters' raised voices.

"Trouble," Dolly said, nodding to the other room as she dipped her spoon into some plain vanilla this time.

"Earplugs?" Charlie asked hopefully. "For two?"

"Sure thing. I got some. Need them in this house with them three harping and banging and who knows what else." She stopped for a moment to listen to the two sisters fight about who was going to play next for Mr. Royale. "But the playing part might be all over for the night. Anyhow, you can have anything I've got, earplugs included. What's mine is yours, always has been."

"What's mine is yours, too, you know that." Charlie smiled widely at her friend. They'd had that pact for years now.

Dolly waved her spoon in the direction of the other room. "But did you have to go and share them three? That I coulda done without."

"What? And let me keep all that pain and suffering to myself?"

They both laughed at that.

When they'd calmed down, Dolly said with a conspiratorial whisper, "But he's a handsome one, ain't he?"

"Oh, my yes." Charlie nearly moaned out her approval.

"Not at all like them pictures of him you see in the papers. Even the ones with him at his island getaway. Much better looking, if you ask me."

"And not as stuck-up as I'd thought."

"Stuck-up?" Alexander Royale asked, standing with a shoulder against the doorframe, arms folded over that wide chest, and his feet crossed at the ankles.

Charlie gulped.

# CHAPTER 3

Alex's breath hitched as he stared at the woman across the room. Her tongue darted out to take a swipe of something from the corner of her mouth. He groaned. She had no idea what she did to a man. Maybe that was the fascination he had with her. He shook his head, trying to dislodge that little tidbit from his mind.

He pushed away from the door and walked toward them. "Ladies, for shame, hiding in here." Then he smiled, saying, "And without telling me and trying to save me from that racket. I'm sure I've lost part of my hearing."

The ladies giggled like schoolgirls, which just seemed to endear them to him even more. If he'd had his way, he'd have spent the entire evening in here with them.

"Mr. R., why don't you grab a spoon and join us? Two drawers over there, you got it," Dolly offered. "Pull up a chair and sit a spell."

He smiled again as he shrugged off his jacket and tossed it on the nearby counter. Pulling out the chair, he turned it around. He straddled it. Taking off his cuff links, he rolled up his sleeves, and then loosened his tie. He looked at the three tall white containers lined in front of him. His mouth watered. "My, my, what do we have here?"

"Dolly's homemade ice cream, at your service." Charlie waved a hand with a flourish. "The best darn ice cream in town."

Turning to her quickly, he gazed directly into her eyes. Soft, warm caramel, he thought. He could get lost in them. Mentally shaking himself, he arched an eyebrow. "The best, huh?"

"Ten bucks says it is." He caught the wink she gave her friend.

"A betting woman."

"Only on a sure thing."

Rubbing his thumb and forefinger over his jaw, he said, "I don't know. Dolly's already proved she's a great cook. Most men wouldn't bet money against a sure thing."

Dolly broke in, saying, "You could put up something other than money."

"Dolly!" Charlie exclaimed.

The maid stared at her wide-eyed. "Not *that*, honey."

Alex bit the inside of his cheek. The two of them could be a comedy team. That was it, he thought; they made him laugh. He couldn't remember the last time he'd laughed as much in a week, never mind just one evening.

"Ten bucks it is then." He pulled out a ten to lay it down on the table.

"Two fives, please," Charlie said.

He frowned, but took out the two fives instead.

"Deal is, all three have to be the best. If they are you get ten bucks. And if not..." He let the last hang in the air as he stared at her parted lips. "A kiss."

"From Dolly," she said with a smile and raised eyebrow.

He took the bait and gave some back. He glanced from Charlie to the maid and back again. "Both of you."

Dolly whooped at that one. "Dagnabbit, I wish I wasn't such a good cook."

Alex chuckled. "Remember, never bet against a sure thing."

A few minutes later, after having tasted all three, he savored the rich flavors melting on his tongue. "No doubt about it, you've won, hands down."

Charlie clapped. She picked up the money. Splitting it, she gave her friend half. "Here's the money I owe you from my bet."

Surprised, Alex asked, "What? You bet against her?"

"Yeah, but I got my money back," Charlie said, waving a five in front of him.

He laughed and the two ladies soon followed suit.

Charlie grabbed a nearby napkin and leaned toward him. "Here, let me."

As she raised her hand to his mouth, he clasped her wrist. She stilled. He heard the catch in her breath. The delicate silky skin beneath his fingers had him yearning to touch more. The vein he lightly pressed changed its rhythm from a slow, steady beat to a rapid-fire tempo.

Gazing at her face, he watched her eyes darken, her cheeks pinken, and her full rosy lips part. Her breath came in soft pants. Something tightened in his middle. An ache rushed through him.

The moment seemed frozen for him. Silence stretched. He felt his own skin heat. Blood throbbed through his veins. His quickening heartbeat drummed in his chest.

Recalling what she'd been about to do, Alex licked the corner of his mouth. She sucked in a breath, dropping her gaze there. He watched in awe at her heavy-lidded stare, the slight flare to her nostrils, and the flush creeping over her cheeks. Another ache, low and deep, shot through him.

From behind him, he heard someone clearing her throat rather loudly and repeatedly.

Coming out of his trance, he said, "Ah, Mrs. King..." There was unmistakable regret in his voice.

He slid his fingers from Charlie's wrist to her palm. She released the napkin she held. Skin met skin. Alex couldn't ignore the tingle traveling through him. He bent and placed a gentle kiss on the back of her hand. Her fingers tightened slightly. Reluctantly, he let her go. He rose.

Straightening the chair, he then moved to Dolly and kissed the back of her hand. "Ladies," he said softly as he turned to Charlie, "it's been memorable." With a slight bow of his head, he turned to face the rest of the pack.

Alex snatched up his jacket from the counter and crossed the room. "Mrs. King, I'll be in touch." As he rolled down his sleeves, he turned to the sisters and nodded. "Girls."

"But… but…" Mrs. King stammered, following on his heels as he found his way to the foyer. "When will you call?" He was sure she sounded desperate even to her own ears.

At the door, he turned to her as he shrugged on his jacket. Tall and proud, she seemed in complete control. However, looking closer, he noted how she rubbed her fingers together and how she couldn't quite disguise the way her eyes clouded with anxiety.

"Tomorrow. First thing. I'll meet you at your office at King's." With that, he left quickly.

The cool air hit Alex the minute he stepped out of the house. At the bottom of the stairs, he halted, raising his face to the soft, misty rain. He smiled.

"Sir?" his driver asked from the curb as he held an umbrella in one hand and pulled the car door open with the other.

"Edward," he said jubilantly, and then raced down the walkway to the car. "It's a wonderful evening, isn't it?"

The older man tipped his black cap. His smile lit up his wizened face. "Yes, sir, it appears it is."

Once in the back seat, Alex grabbed for the car phone. As he waited several rings, Edward pulled the car out into the street.

"Hello," came a sleepy male voice.

"Granddad, it's Alex."

"Alex! Is everything all right, son?"

Alex laughed out loud. "Granddad, I found her."

He found her, but would she want him and a marriage of convenience?

# CHAPTER 4

From behind the wheel of the car, Edward glanced over his shoulder. "Is she the one who was late, sir? Dark hair, slender, long legs? She ran across the street while laughing in the pouring rain."

Nodding, Alex smiled at his longtime friend's description. He couldn't believe it had only been last night since he met her. He hadn't slept a wink. He'd replayed the time with her over and over in his mind. But one nagging thought persisted. Who the hell was Dex? A boyfriend? Was it serious?

Now he waited outside King's Department Store for Charlie's arrival. He glanced at his watch, realizing they'd been parked there for more than ten minutes. Well, he hadn't wanted to miss her.

"Sir, I think she's coming now," Edward said as he gazed in the rearview mirror.

Alex twisted around and spotted her. Her dark hair gleamed in the morning light. Wearing a short, purple dress that hugged her curves and matching high heels, she walked down the sidewalk. He turned to his friend and patted him on the shoulder. "Good job, Edward. Wish me luck."

A moment later, Alex hopped out of the car, not bothering to wait for his driver. Charlie walked briskly by, but not without a double take when she saw him.

He smiled. Maybe he had a chance. Following a few paces behind her, he watched her long, self-assured strides and the gentle sway of her backside. "Damn," he muttered, straightening his jacket, and then buttoned it.

She must have heard because he caught her soft chuckle. It probably wasn't the first time and it wouldn't be the last time a man commented as she strode down the street, he figured.

\*\*\*

Charlie nearly lost her footing when Alex stepped from the limo at the curb, never in her life expecting him to emerge from the sleek, black car. Now he was no more than four steps behind her, watching her. She took guilty pleasure in his muttered compliment, warmth spreading across her cheeks.

Once at the gold-framed glass doors of King's, she smiled widely at the short, older doorman as he held the door for her. "Benny, how are you today? And how's your new granddaughter, Andrea?"

His wrinkled face stretched with his smile and his blue eyes twinkled with delight. "She's just a peach,

Miss Charlie. Thanks so much for the bassinet. It's a beauty."

"I'm so glad you liked it. Don't forget to bring some pictures of her. We want to make sure she's on King's family board."

"Sure thing, miss. You have a good day now."

She sensed Alex still followed her. However, her suspicions were confirmed when Benny wished him a good morning and he responded in his deep, rich voice.

Glancing back quickly, she caught him staring at her. A shiver of awareness shot through her middle. Without missing a step, she walked across the charcoal gray marble floor. She strode past the men's department, cosmetics counter, and jewelry department. Charlie headed to the executive offices' elevators.

Usually she took her time surveying the scene and filling with pride. Today, the man behind her distracted her, making it difficult to think of anything but his strong presence.

Halting at the gleaming gold doors, she saw him stop a foot behind her. "Good morning." She nodded to the three people already waiting. Two men from their accounting department returned her pleasantries.

In the muted reflection, Charlie caught Alex staring. She turned her head, saying, "Quit following."

"Why? I like the view from back here." His voice held an unmistakable smile.

The others chuckled. Charlie grinned and shook her head. Thankfully, the door dinged opened. Entering, she found a spot in the center, and then turned back to the doors. Once again, he followed and stood just inches behind her. The others piled in beside them.

Thick silence ensued as the doors closed and the elevator lifted them to the fifth floor. The heat from his body reached out to scorch her back. His musky scent tickled her senses. Momentarily, she closed her eyes and breathed in. Why did she have to be attracted to this man? He's Francie's.

She must have swayed slightly; his hand touched her waist to steady her. Charlie opened her eyes quickly.

He murmured in her ear, "Are you all right?" His warm breath fanned over her earlobe and neck. She shivered.

All she could do was nod. His fingers lingered. The heat of his touch burned through her clothes, branding her flesh. Slowly, he dropped his hand, his palm brushing her hip. His sharp intake of breath whistled past her ear.

An eternity later, the elevator halted at her floor. She rushed out, gulping in air, and greeted the receptionist. "Good morning, Martha."

"Hi, Charlie."

Charlie made her escape from Alex, striding to the right and toward her corner office. Behind her, she heard him ask for Mrs. King. "Of course," she whispered, "he's here to talk about last night and Francie." Her middle tightened.

\*\*\*

Still dizzy from his encounter with Charlie, Alex was ushered into Mrs. King's office. He noted the ornately carved desk and the rich burgundy fabric on the furniture.

The older woman grabbed his attention. She stood with confidence. Dressed in a black tailored business suit, her dyed golden hair swept in a French twist and a string of creamy pearls around her neck, she exuded professionalism.

"Mrs. King." He nodded politely, sizing up the woman more closely than the night before. There was something about her…

Shrewd, dark eyes narrowed slightly, as if trying to read his thoughts. She pasted on a smile. "Why, Mr. Royale, it's such a pleasure."

Somehow he doubted that, especially when he told her of his intentions.

After she finished with the pleasantries of coffee and her secretary left the room, she began, "We had such a lovely evening with you."

Alex had two options: Either he could go along with this charade or cut to the chase. "Mrs. King, we both know why I'm here."

"Yes." Nudging her cup and saucer aside, she pushed away the pretense. She leaned forward in her chair, her hands grasped tightly together. He was certain she held her breath.

"Your daughter-"

"Francine," she interrupted, relaxing her hands. "I knew it. She's a lovely girl. Quite a catch."

"Not that one."

Her brow furrowed and she looked genuinely puzzled. "Priscilla?"

"Not that one, either."

"But...but who?" Then her jaw slackened and her eyes widened.

"Yes, that one."

"Charlotte!" Her mouth opened and closed.

He stifled a laugh at her shocked look. "It's not a problem, is it?"

He knew she'd never be able to refuse. If she turned Alexander Royale down for a chance to marry one of her daughters, it would get out and her reputation would be shredded to pieces. Now, Charlie's acceptance may be an entirely different story. A fusion of doubt shot through him.

Visibly trying to pull herself together, she smoothed a hand over her perfectly styled hair. She relaxed her mouth into a semblance of a smile. "No, of course it's not a problem. Not at all."

"She's available then?" He held his breath.

She waved a hand and made a sound in the back of her throat. "Dexter Snodgrass? Oh, he's nothing, just one of our mad scientists. You know the type, always concocting one thing or another. Perfume this time..." She rambled off.

"Good." Alex could breathe again, the tightening in his chest easing. But he had a feeling she wanted something out of this. "The terms?"

She sat up, straightening her back. Her eyes brightened. "Now, you know, she is a King." Somehow she'd regained complete composure. "Nothing but the best."

"Of course." His middle clenched. Alex kept a snare from forming on his lips at the change in this woman. She'd barely tolerated Charlie last night.

"I don't know if you're aware of this or not, Mr. Royale, but I was given the right to accept or deny any of Charlotte's suitors for her hand in marriage. In his will, her father entrusted me with the responsibility." She raised her chin and cocked her head to the side.

Alex balled his fingers into a fist. "And if she goes against your wishes?" he asked between gritted teeth.

"She'll be disowned. Disinherited. Cut off from her family. Kicked out of the store. No contact with the store employees she loves. Left with nothing. Not even a stick of furniture." He swore he saw a ghost of a smile cross her lips.

"Mr. King put that in his will?" Alex kept a tight control on his voice, wishing to give nothing away to this cold, hard woman.

"King's was quite the store back then. *The store*. We had lots of interest in it and it was very profitable. We had to protect us, the store, and the girls from any untoward influences or unsavory characters. My husband left the consequences up to me." This time she did let the smile linger.

"And it still stands to this day?"

"It's ironclad. I wouldn't have had it any other way."

Barracuda was too kind of a word to describe this woman. "What's your price, Mrs. King?" He wanted to get this over with; he couldn't stand to sit in the same room with her a moment longer than necessary.

"King's."

He wasn't certain he heard right. "King's Department Store?"

"Yes. I want it sold. Either you buy it or find the highest bidder. You'll be in charge once you marry the girl. The employees will love that. The late, great Charles King's beloved daughter takes a husband. Anything to please the poor orphaned Charlotte King and her legacy." Venom laced her words. "It should be easy for you to sway them eventually. You can use your powers of persuasion. I hear you're quite the fireball in boardrooms, fighting and winning your way."

If he felt disgust before, it was nothing like the hard stone sitting in his belly now. "You hate her that much?" he asked tightly. How could anyone dislike beautiful, fun-loving Charlie?

He swore he saw a hint of moisture clouding her eyes. "It's difficult to compete with your husband's child. She was always his favorite—" Her voice caught. She made a sound in the back of her throat. Her eyes cleared into two hard chips of ice. "Do we have a deal, Mr. Royale?"

"What do you get out of it?" He wanted to know.

"Freedom," she nearly hissed. "This store has been an albatross around my neck. That and my husband's ghost filling this store, twisting the employees' heads to him, hoarding their loyalty on a dead man."

"Of course, you'll end up a very rich woman," he baited, realizing the truth of the rumors he'd heard about the store's falling earnings over the last few quarters. If she sold it in the near future she'd still see a tidy profit. The longer she held on, the more the store lost, and the lower her take.

But to buy a failing store? How could he justify it, to himself, to his granddad? Royale Enterprises, the family business, focused on developing property, a dream full of hope and promise. They were not in the market of taking over an existing operation to try to shore up a quickly plummeting bottom line.

His curiosity won out. "Why not sell it yourself?"

"And be more of a villain than I already am?" She recoiled. "I know what they say about me. If I'm ever to keep my head up in this town, then I must not be the one to do all the dirty work."

Silently, he agreed. The society she clung to would oust her from the fringes of their circle.

"Despite what you've heard, Mr. Royale, I am a very smart woman. I intend to come out on top, the belle of the ball, so to speak, and with a load of money to boot."

The room grew even colder for Alex. Charlie and the girls were just as much a commodity to this woman as the store was. Everything had a dollar sign on it for her.

Last night he'd met Charlie, a woman who'd made him laugh, made him step outside his comfort level. Also, she made him think that he could find a wife who didn't want to follow all those strict, imposed rules and become a carbon copy society wife who would bore him to death.

When Charlie bumped into him, she'd turned his world upside down. And his emotions.

In less than a minute, she'd exposed his lonely existence, sparking a need he didn't even know he had. He longed for more than just a marriage of convenience. He wanted a wife, in every sense of the word.

He wanted her. But at what price?

He weighed his options and made his final decision.

Standing up, he watched Mrs. King follow suit. "King's Department Store in exchange for Charlie, is that it?"

"Exactly," she murmured with a sly smile.

Grim determination took hold. He'd sell the damn thing and be done with it. He held out his hand. "You have a deal."

# CHAPTER 5

Leaning against the doorframe to Charlie's charming little corner office with large windows and cozy window seats beneath them, Alex could finally breathe fresh air again. The arctic room and woman he'd just left was now replaced with warmth and a sense of peace at seeing Charlie and her surroundings. He watched her at her desk with her head bent over her work. She drew something that held her rapt attention.

Tendrils of her dark hair fell forward. She brushed them back impatiently. Her teeth gnawed at her bottom lip as she swept the charcoal pencil over the half-filled page. He imagined soothing that tortured flesh.

Tenderness welled up inside him.

How in the world had she survived with that cold hearted, emotionless woman as her stepmother all these years? But she had. And thrived, if his guess was correct from all her laughter and high jinks of the night before and even this morning. A well of admiration pooled inside of him. God, she was so adorable.

The phone rang. "Can you get that, Peg?" she asked, never taking her focus off the page. "Tell them I'm busy and will call them back."

Peg, he assumed, was her secretary. However, she'd stepped away from her desk. The shrill ring sounded again. He strolled in, snatching up her phone. She looked up. Her eyes widened and her hand stilled.

"Hello, this is Miss King's office." He heard a voice utter a sound, but didn't let them say anything. "She's unable to take any calls right now. Can you please call back this afternoon?"

"Who's this?" a male voice asked.

Alex frowned. "Who's this?"

"Dexter. Is Charlie there?"

He let out a slow breath. "Dexter." He glanced at Charlie and watched a flush creep over her cheeks. His middle tightened. Did she have feelings for the man? Ones her stepmother weren't aware of?

Doubt nagged at him. Would she agree to marry him?

Reluctantly, he held out the receiver toward her, raising his eyebrows. She stared at the black instrument, and then back at him. While biting her lip, she slowly shook her head. He breathed a sigh of relief.

Maybe he had a chance.

Alex pulled the receiver back to his ear. "She's unavailable." He took guilty pleasure in saying that. If he had his way about it Charlie would be unavailable very shortly.

A muttered curse blast in his ear. A sudden dial tone echoed.

Good-bye to you, too, he thought, and then replaced the phone in its cradle.

"Alex!"

He liked the breathy sound of her voice, the way it caught on his name. "Charlie," he said softly, watching her pupils flare with awareness. He leaned a hip on her desk.

She glanced down. "Why don't you make yourself comfortable?"

"Thanks, I will." He smiled widely. Gazing at the paper she'd been sketching on, he reached over and plucked it up, turning it toward him. He had no idea what he'd expected, but certainly not this. "Me?"

Red spread over her cheeks and she snatched the drawing away from him. "It's... ah... research. I'm thinking of doing a fairy-tale window display." She quickly sketched in short, quick strokes. In a matter of seconds, she'd fashioned a jewel-encrusted crown on his head. "Ah... who better than Prince Charming to adorn it?"

He searched her gaze, slowly and intently. Her caramel eyes gave nothing away. "Really?"

Shrugging, she said, "I'm the art director. I have to come up with hundreds of ideas."

"Ah, then you're just the one for me," he said, entirely serious.

She gulped. "Really? What would you need my ideas for? I mean, surely, you have your own people who can come up with something." She frowned. "And what kind of ideas are we talking about?"

"It's personal. A job only you can do. Have lunch with me today and I'll tell you."

"But, it's only—" she stopped, grabbed his wrist and turned it to read the face of his gold Rolex. "Quarter to ten."

She pulled her hand away before he could stop her. But the soft, velvety touch lingered on. He shook his head slightly, trying to regain his thoughts. "I'll send my driver, Edward, for you at noon." He got up and strode for the door.

"But I haven't accepted yet," she called out.

He halted, turning to her with a smile and raised eyebrow.

"Personal? Can't you give me even a little hint?"

"Prince Charming takes a wife," he said, winking at her. Her gasp of surprise followed him down the hallway.

# CHAPTER 6

Charlie waited for the driver to settle into traffic before she climbed onto the facing rich, buttery leather seat. The glass partition was open. She leaned forward. "Limo, huh?"

"Town car's in the shop."

"Edward, right?"

Smiling, he gazed in the rearview mirror. He shifted his uniform cap slightly, and then said, "At your service."

Kind hazel eyes twinkled in his square face. He had a nice wide smile, which helped ease her anxiety somewhat.

Nudging his shoulder, she said, "So tell me which one did he pick?"

"Ma'am?"

"Prince Charming."

"Mr. Royale?" He chuckled, visibly relaxing. "Is that what you call him to his face?"

"Yep. It's the truth, isn't it?" She caught his knowing grin in the mirror's reflection.

He remained quiet, so she nudged him again. "Come on, you have to know everything that goes on. Which one did he pick?" This was good news for the store, right? So why was she tied up in knots?

Her stepmother had dodged her all morning. Charlie hadn't been privy to whatever she and Alex had discussed. Her nerves were working overtime.

He darted a glance over his shoulder. "You don't know?"

"Was it Francine?" Charlie nearly cringed at the crack in her voice. Half of her hoped it was, but the other half prayed it wasn't.

"That the older one?" he asked, appearing cautious.

"It is her!" Dread pooled in her middle. How in the world could she ever be Alex's sister-in-law?

"Didn't say that," he said, hastening to correct her.

"Priscilla? No way! She barely said five words last night." She chewed her bottom lip. "Unless he likes them quiet. Is that it, he likes the quiet, shy type?"

There was no hope for her. She mentally kicked herself. What was she thinking anyway? Alex wouldn't be interested in her. She wasn't the cool, sophisticated society wife that he obviously needed by his side.

Of course, she wasn't even interested in marriage.

And then there was Dex... A twinge of guilt shot through her. She'd barely thought of her friend since she'd left his lab late yesterday and after he'd called earlier. Deep down, she sensed his feelings were more involved, more than two friends sharing their passion for work and saving the store.

"Ma'am, you're jumping to conclusions now."

Another thought struck her. "Well, if it's Stepmother, I think you ought to have the man committed."

"I'd drive him there myself and make sure he doesn't come out for a long, long time."

They both laughed at that. Charlie now knew that Alex had to have told Edward at least some of the details of the King family. Just how much she couldn't be sure.

"You're not going to tell me, are you, Edward?"

"No, ma'am."

She sighed. "In spite of it, I still like you." That gave her another idea. "Hey, are you available?"

"For you?" His voice sounded puzzled.

"Not me, silly," she said, lightly swatting him on the shoulder. "My friend, Dolly."

Twenty minutes later, after having extolled Dolly's virtues to the interested man, he pulled into the marina.

"Fishing? Is that his idea of lunch?" she muttered under her breath.

Edward must have heard; he chuckled as he came around the car to open her door.

The warm balmy lake breeze caressed her face as she stepped out into the sunlight. Closing her eyes, she breathed in deeply, smelling the tangy air. She murmured her approval.

"Like it?" Alex's question tugged her out of her reverie.

Opening her eyes, she followed his voice. He stood on the pier with his hands on his hips, wearing worn tight jeans and a low-buttoned white shirt. She sucked in a sharp breath. "Yes, I like it very much." She skipped the details on just exactly what she liked.

His driver helped her negotiate the parking area and the wooden planks of the pier. "Thanks, Edward." She gazed behind Alex at the tall, gallant white vessel. Looking at him again, she said, "My, what a big boat you have, Mr. Royale."

His easy grin slid across his face. Alex waited at the bottom of the stairs. He bowed, and then raised a hand to the hulking ship. "Your chariot awaits, my lady."

She giggled, liking his playful manner. He wasn't the stuck-up businessman she'd assumed he was.

Holding out a hand, he guided her down to his level.

She stepped in close, bumping him slightly. "Oops," she said, looking up into his twinkling brown eyes. Trying to step back, she felt his hands hold her waist lightly.

For long, silent minutes he gazed down at her. The intense stare mesmerized Charlie. Finally, she broke the heated contact only to end up glancing at his lips. They were moving, saying something, but she couldn't be certain what since all the blood had rushed to her ears.

Shaking her head, she said, "I don't understand."

"You will. In time," he whispered back.

Slowly, he released her, and Charlie wasn't sure if her shaky legs would cooperate and move. But he helped her down the last of the pier and up into the awaiting yacht.

Gleaming blonde wood and the soft lap of water hitting the side of the vessel greeted her. Within minutes, he introduced her to the crew and asked if she'd like a tour.

Looking down at her feet, he said, "You may want to trade those in. Heels aren't exactly the best form of transportation on a moving yacht."

She followed his gaze, and then looked at his bare feet. "What is it with you and the shoes, anyway?" she asked. Gingerly, she slipped out of her heels. She carefully rolled down her thigh high stockings, highly aware of his intent stare and low murmur of approval. "Ta-dah," she said, pulling the stockings free and whisking them through her hands to straighten them.

"Here, let me," he said, holding out his hand.

With a shrug, she handed them over and watched as he tucked them into his shirt pocket, part of the nylon poking out.

She grinned. "Nice touch."

"Like it? It's the latest fashion trend."

They both chuckled. He held out his hand. "My lady…"

She smiled widely, slipping her hand in his large, warm grasp.

As they made their way through the cabins below, Charlie couldn't help but ooh and aah over the rich, mahogany wood, gold outfittings, and plush furnishings. Mr. Alexander Royale was definitely living large.

Finally, he led her up to the wide, long deck. The warm wood beneath her feet and the afternoon sunlight bathing her skin had Charlie relaxing instantly. His large hand clasping hers made her feel safe and cared for.

Stop that, she scolded herself; he's Francie's. But he hadn't said it yet, hadn't burst any bubbles yet.

Just this once, this moment, she promised herself, she'd enjoy his company.

He halted near the bow of the yacht where a laden table awaited with sparkling crystal and pristine white china. A small bouquet of colorful flowers adorned the center.

Holding out a chair for her, he said, "Charlie."

She smiled, feeling pampered. "Alex," she murmured. His low, soft chuckle teased her ear.

Seating himself across from her, he nodded to his waiting chef. Soon trays of food were brought before them. As the platters appeared, Charlie's tummy rumbled at the mouth-watering grilled salmon and mixed vegetables.

Alex chatted. Charlie kept up her side of the conversation throughout the meal. But in the back of her mind she recalled why she was here. He wanted Francie for his wife. The nagging thought dampened her spirits. She couldn't hide that fact any longer. The food melted in her mouth, but, when it sank to her middle, it hit like a rock, hard and sharp. A sip of water stuck in her suddenly dry throat.

As her mind echoed, *He's Francie's, he's Francie's*, her stomach knotted even more. Perspiration trickled down her forehead. She swiped at it.

"Are you all right?" His concern only made her insides twist more.

Taking a deep breath, she said, "I'll be fine. Maybe we just need to get down to business."

He raised his left eyebrow. "Business?"

Dabbing a napkin on her upper lip, she said, "Yes, remember, you needed my ideas. I take it it's for your bride." The last word stuck and faltered. She cleared her throat, her voice stronger now. "Is it the dress? Between my designs and Dolly, who's a whiz on a sewing machine, well, let's just say if we were in business together we'd be giving some people a run for their money."

Of course, that's why he invited her here today. Her stepmother must have championed her and Dolly as the dressmakers. But when did her stepmother ever praise her? And why would a groom care about a wedding dress?

Her head seemed light on her shoulders, her thoughts harder to grasp and hold on to. Looking at him across the table, she made a concerted effort to blink away the white spots swimming between them and focus on those gorgeous dark eyes of his.

He nudged his nearly full glass of wine toward her and waited while she took a long, deep sip. "A dress?"

Her head cleared slightly. "Yes, no offense, but Francie does need some help in the fashion department. Well, she's a genius when it comes to ballet." She stopped herself short, frowning. "Did I tell you she's an incredible ballerina? Such talent. She would have went all the way, too, if—"

"Her mother hadn't nixed it, right?"

"You know her so well. But don't let Stepmother stop you. Francie's like a little caterpillar. She's cocooning now, but soon she'll be the most beautiful butterfly."

Charlie's middle clenched tightly. Nausea bubbled up to her throat. She swallowed hard, stumping it down. She tried another gulp of wine, hoping it would relax the grippers. She looked anxiously at the side railing to her right and farthest away from Alex. Then she turned back to look at him again.

"You speak highly of her."

"Why not? She's talented. Some of it, the little bits of it, she's found, but someday she'll uncover so many more treasures to behold. That's when she'll blossom."

He rubbed his jaw. "Blossom?"

"Yes," she croaked out, grabbing for the wine glass once again.

"You're so sure. Unwavering loyalty, Charlie?"

A dull heat swept over her cheeks. She bowed her eyes and shook her head. "No." She shrugged uncomfortably. "I can spot talent when I see it."

"See any lately?" His soft voice wrapped around her center.

She sucked in a sharp breath, catching and holding his stare. "Maybe... I've recently met a prince, of all things. The most charming man."

He leaned closer, covering her hand. "Really?"

Feeling the rumble in her middle before she heard it, Charlie dragged her hand away and pressed it to her tummy.

His brow furrowed. "Charlie, you're under a misconception here."

"How so? Have you gotten me here under false pretenses?" She tried to make her voice light and cheery, but it fell flat.

He dragged a hand down his face and sighed. "Something like that."

Another cramp seized her middle. "Explain, please," she squeaked out.

Looking directly at her now, he said softly, "It's not Francine I want for a bride."

Charlie shook her head. "Priscilla?" she barely whispered.

"No."

Her stomach ached. Maybe it wasn't even someone she knew. Either way, she didn't think she wanted to hear his answer, but she had to ask anyway. Breathing in short, quick breaths, she asked, "Someone else? Who?"

He seemed to force a smile as his frown deepened. "You, Charlie," he said softly. "Will you marry me?"

Just then her belly heaved. She shoved back her chair, the legs painfully scraping against the wood, and dashed to the side railing. Leaning over, she'd made it just in time.

# CHAPTER 7

Alex dragged a hand through his hair as he paced back and forth in his large, echoing foyer. "Is she all right? Did you get her home safely?" He couldn't squelch the anxiety in his voice.

"Sir, she was a little pale and shaky, but she'll be fine. You said you called her friend, Dolly, didn't you?" When Alex gave him a nod, he went on, "So there you have it. She'll sort Miss Charlie out."

"I can't believe she took it so badly. It couldn't have come as that much of a shock. Surely she had to know I was attracted to her."

"Denial."

Halting, Alex looked over his shoulder at his driver. "Denial? How so?" Frowning, he began pacing again. "I never once made any overtures to either one of the other sisters. Never a hint of attraction or even interest in either one of them. Nothing for her to think it was Francine or even Priscilla. No, it was always her." He shook his head.

"It's her, sir. She didn't want to see it. Probably had her mind set on someone else and boom, you hit her with it." He shrugged his shoulders. "So, I wouldn't take it personal- her getting sick. Shock was all it was."

Alex halted in front of his friend. Letting out a weary breath, he tried to allow it to sink in. "I should go to her. Try to explain things."

This time it was Edward who frowned. "Not everything, sir. Surely not everything."

The skin on his face felt even tighter as he caught and held his driver's concerned gaze. "No, Edward, I can't tell her that." Heaviness seemed to weigh down his body, sinking deeper and deeper. "From what I can gather, that store means the world to her. I think it would destroy her if she knew what I was about to do with it."

"You could always call it off."

His chest tightened. "Not likely, Edward. After all this time, I finally found a woman I'm willing to marry. So much is at risk here. If I keep my word about King's, I hurt Charlie but honor my grandparents' wishes by marrying and later producing the heir they desperately crave."

"Tough choice."

"The business or Charlie."

"No, sir, the way I see it is, it's your grandparents or Miss Charlie."

\*\*\*

"There now, honey," Dolly soothed, patting her on the shoulder. "It ain't that bad."

Charlie raised her head from her hands and moaned. "You didn't ever throw up when someone asked you to marry him, did you?"

Dolly chuckled. "No, can't say I ever did that." She winked, saying, "But I've done some pretty silly stuff in my day, I'll have you know. My, the stories I could tell…" Her voice trailed off.

"I just bet you could." She sighed heavily.

"Maybe you got seasick, ever think of that?" She wrinkled her nose. "Or even sick from all that rich food, you know. That fancy stuff never set right with you."

"I wish I could blame it on something else." Charlie groaned. "I can't believe I did that. Of all the things in the world to do in front of him, that was the last."

Suddenly, Dolly clapped her hands and whooped, startling Charlie.

Frowning, she looked at her friend. "What? Did I say something funny?"

"You like him, that's all," she said, holding her hands together and grinning broadly.

Warmth spread to her cheeks. "Why do you say that?" She heard the brittle tone in her own voice and cringed at the similarity to her stepmother's demeanor.

"'Cause you wouldn't care a fig if it were anyone else you puked in front of. Not that Dexter, I'll have you know."

Her middle cramped again. She raised her hands to her cheeks. "Dexter?" she barely whispered. "I keep forgetting about him."

"See, if you ever had any real feelings for the science boy wonder, which we both know you don't and never will, you'd have thought of him first thing."

She acknowledged the truth. Their commitment to the store she longed to save created a strong bond and a shared goal. But Dex thought and felt differently. She didn't want to hurt her friend.

Another realization hit her. "But Alexander Royale? He's so unreachable, his world, lifestyle," she threw up her hands, "everything. Why me?"

"Don't you say those kinds of things. He coulda had one of them society wives all along. Did he? Nope. Know why? He's sick to death of them kind, that's why. Probably been offered up on platters to him all his life. He's got sense, that one. Why settle for plain when you can have an original, Charlie?"

Charlie chuckled, shaking her head. "You have such a way with words, my friend. An original, you say?"

Nudging her, Dolly said, "Dag straight, you are. Ain't no two like you, I'll have you know." The kettle whistle blew. "I'll have you some tea in a jiffy. With lots of honey, just like you like it."

A tinge of a smile tugged at her lips. Tea with lots of honey had been her cure-all while growing up. Tea, honey, and Dolly.

"Hey, you know what I was just thinking of?" Dolly's muffled words came from the depths of the kitchenette.

"Oh, no, you've been thinking again." This time she smiled fully.

Dolly rounded the corner and stuck out her tongue at Charlie. "Smart aleck."

Taking a deep, cleansing breath, she shrugged. "Couldn't help it."

Teacups rattled as the maid set the tray on the coffee table. Scooping one up, Charlie sipped the sweet, soothing liquid.

Sitting down beside her friend, Dolly poked Charlie with an elbow. "The thinking part, remember? Why you and I will get to live together after all. You his wife and me his cook, how's them apples?" Her voice went up a little higher in her excitement.

"You're taking it? You're actually going to leave the barracuda for good?"

She got another poke with an elbow. "Damn straight, if you'll be there. It'll be just like we've always dreamed about. You and me. You sketching your dresses and me making them."

"Ah, I hate to burst your bubble, but you'd still have to work for … him." Her voice caught on Alex's name.

"That's the thing. He's paying me double to do half the work I've been doing. Ain't that a hoot?" She put down her cup and clapped her hands in glee. "No more dusting, vacuuming, making beds, cleaning toilets, nothing. He's already got a maid to do all that."

Charlie pulled back slightly. She put down her own cup. A ray of hope for Dolly spread in her middle. "You're sure about this?"

"Had me a good little talk with Mr. R."

"When?"

"This morning. He came around to the house and made me a deal I couldn't refuse. He even had a contract made out and all. Real fancy like."

Charlie's mind raced with the sequence of events. Alex must have gone to see Dolly right after he left her office this morning, and then he went to the yacht for their lunch date. "Did...did he say anything about me then?"

Dolly waved her off with a hand. "Oh, no, he never told me his plans for you. But he did say you could come visit anytime you wanted to, stay as long as you like." She shrugged her shoulders. "You know, giving you free rein of his house."

"So he knew."

"Honey, he knew last night. The way he was looking at you and kissing your hand."

"He kissed yours, too," Charlie pointed out.

She sighed wistfully. "But not like yours."

Leaning over, Dolly bumped her shoulder against Charlie's, and then moved slightly away.

"What do you say, kiddo? You and me living with *the* Alexander Royale? Ain't too shabby for the likes of us."

Regaining her sense of humor, she said, "It does have some interesting possibilities, doesn't it? I don't think he would know what hit him with the pair of us." She giggled as the thoughts tumbled through her mind.

"Do you think we could get him to be our mannequin for our new designs? You know, a little silk here, a little lace there..." She burst out laughing and Charlie joined her.

Suddenly there was a sharp rap on the door, startling Charlie and her friend.

A moment later, taking a deep, shaky breath, Charlie opened the door. "Stepmother! What are you doing here?"

The thin-lipped woman shot her a look of disdain. "Really, Charlotte, your manners." She brushed past Charlie and came to an abrupt halt. Quickly, she gazed around the loft apartment. Her brow furrowed more and more as she took in the tiny, sparsely furnished area. "Really, Charlotte!"

Charlie's middle clenched tightly. The verbal reprimand careened her back to her childhood. To throw her off, she said, "I'm glad you approve."

The air thickened between them. Her stepmother moved into the room, looking from left to right, scanning every element with her shrewd gaze. Turning back to Charlie, she said, "That's not what I meant and you know it. Why do you always have to be so difficult? Your snide comebacks and now this, you getting sick after a marriage proposal from one of the wealthiest men in Dallas."

She reared back, feeling the color drain from her face. "How—"She stopped herself short and twisted to search for Dolly.

Her friend winced, forced a smile, and then said, "Sorry. She called when you were in the bathroom brushing your teeth and changing into jeans. You puking your guts out kinda...slipped out."

Groaning loudly, she wished she could turn back the hands of time and erase this meeting completely. She steeled herself for bad news; surely, her stepmother would reverse her decision to revamp the store now. Gritting her teeth, she asked, "All right, Stepmother, what is it you would like to say?"

Her stepmother's eyebrows shot up, clearly not expecting the question. "Marry him."

"That's it, that's all you have?" She couldn't stop the stunned wonder from entering her voice. What, no reprimand for stealing Francie's prospective groom?

"You're a silly twit if you don't."

"What about Francine and Priscilla?"

For the first time, she looked away and smoothed the back of her French twist. Her lips pursed, and then she said, "He seems to have overlooked them."

Dawning hit Charlie. Alex had met with her stepmother this morning. It had been about her, not one of her stepsisters. How shocking for both her stepmother and her. Charlie had never thought she'd marry. Ever. The family store had always been her top priority.

"And you don't care? I mean, him picking me over them?" She knew she shouldn't have made the comparison.

Her stepmother dropped her hand and straightened her spine. Staring intently at her, she said, "He chose a King and for that you should be proud. You want the legacy to live on, don't you? Here's your chance to have all you ever wanted—"She stopped abruptly.

Hope filled Charlie's middle. She blinked several times, trying to absorb it all. "You mean, if I marry him, you'll agree to the changes I want to make at King's? The changes we talked about last night after dinner?"

Her mouth tightened. Finally, she said, "Let's just say that I have every intention of making a profit in the near future."

"King's, you mean."

"What else could I mean?" she asked, avoiding her stare.

Why didn't Charlie feel completely comfortable with her answer? Nothing had ever been this easy with the woman who controlled the purse strings for the store. Could she trust her stepmother to keep her word? More importantly, could she really marry Alexander Royale, Prince Charming?

# CHAPTER 8

Charlie roamed his large house with Alex following at a discreet pace. Each room was fashionably decorated with the most exquisite taste in furnishings. Leather chairs, rich woods, and creamy white walls greeted her. But she didn't feel it was a home, just a building with expensive things showcased. Her mind raced with possibilities of redecorating. Warmth, light, and color, she thought; that's what the place needed.

She entered his cozy study once again, feeling welcome here. This room seemed warmer to her. It gave her more of a glimpse into the man who wanted to marry her.

As if sensing her thoughts, Alex said, "It's yours to do with as you please." An unmistakable softness entered his voice. "I want you to be happy and feel at home."

She whispered under her breath, "I haven't said yes yet."

He chuckled. "No, you haven't. That could be a bone of contention, now wouldn't it?"

Trying to hide her smile, she turned to him with raised eyebrows. "Or we could skip the marriage part altogether. I could just decorate for you. Get this place spiffed up, roam the halls—"

"And drive me crazy." He laughed, but his eyes darkened to a warm chocolate brown.

She sucked in a sharp breath. Her middle tightened. He certainly knew how to get to her. All he had to do was look at her like that and she was a goner. In the back of her mind, she wondered how many other times he used that look and on how many other women.

Moving a step nearer, he closed the small space between them. He brushed back a lock of her hair, his fingertips skimming her cheek. Her heart skipped a beat.

"Sweet Charlie," he murmured, his warm breath fanning her lips.

She shivered. "Alex," she whispered. "I don't even know you." She spoke her thoughts out loud.

"That part will change."

"Now or later?"

"Later."

"What if I don't like you?"

A quick smile lit up his face. "What if I don't like you?" He tossed the question back at her.

"That's impossible, everyone loves me," she said cheekily.

He chuckled. "Even the barracuda?"

She grimaced. "Okay, everybody but her, how's that?"

Right before her eyes, his smile faded and his face sobered. He stepped back. "What about Dexter? Is he in love with you? Are you in love with him?" The last came out between gritted teeth.

Charlie swallowed hard. "Yes and no." The words stuck in her throat. A wave of remorse washed through her. She never intended to mislead Dex. Somehow, she thought he'd feel that way anyway.

Frowning, Alex gazed at her. "Yes for what part and no for what part of the question?"

Taking a shaky breath, she answered, "Yes he loves me, in his own way, and no I don't love him."

He let out a big sigh and the lines on his face relaxed. "Well, that's good to know."

"What about you? Involved?"

"Hardly."

"The women in the paper?"

"Dates."

"And prospective brides."

"Hardly," he repeated, this time with a crisp edge to the word.

She took a deep, shuttering breath. "Why me?"

He hesitated. "You're the only one I wanted."

The low timber of his voice and the darkening of his eyes tugged at her middle. Her breath came in short, shallow puffs. "I…I don't know what to say."

A smile twitched at the corner of his mouth. "Yes would be the preferred choice."

Chuckling, she shook her head. "You are persistent."

Just then she heard footsteps coming toward them. "Oh, my, ain't this something, honey?" Dolly drew near and nudged her arm. "Edward's been showing me around. He's a teddy bear." She winked and made a low sound in her throat. "I can't wait to get started. You gotta see the kitchen. It's to die for."

Charlie looked at Alex. His long, lingering gaze sent warmth through her. He whispered, "It's to die for."

"The house or you?" she asked under her breath.

"Me, of course."

She chuckled. Out of the corner of her eye, she noticed Dolly motioning to Alex. Her friend slipped something into the drawer of a small table nestled between two chairs. He looked puzzled.

Dolly straightened. She smoothed her hands over her pretty blue dress. She glanced from Charlie to Alex and back to Charlie again. "I'm interrupting you two love-birds, ain't I?"

"Yes," Alex said.

"No," Charlie said.

"Tell you what, Mr. R., if it's okay with you, I'll just whip up something quick for dinner while you and Miss Charlie finish the details."

Turning quickly to her friend, she said, "Dolly!"

"No need to thank me, honey." She winked again and rushed out of the room.

"Shall we?" Alex asked, waving a hand to the chairs flanking the small table.

Her heartbeat quickened.

Moving across the room, she felt a sharp pang. His study brought back a rush of sweet memories of her father's drawing room. Rows and rows of leather-bound books on the shelves, a large oak desk with his papers neatly stacked in the center...

Sitting in the deep leather chair, Charlie felt instantly at home. She tried to shake off the piercing ache of need shooting through her, but she failed miserably.

She'd never had any longings for anything remotely close to a long-term relationship, never mind a marriage.

The more time she spent with Alex, the more glimpses she had of what she could have: a husband, a marriage, eventually children. And the more her heart tugged for what she thought she never wanted.

Perched on the edge of the chair, she twisted to him as he sat back in the matching chair on the other side of the small, round chess table.

Arching an eyebrow, he nodded to her.

"Why me first?" She sounded childish to her own ears.

"I already know what I want."

His dark, hungry gaze made her shiver. There was something about him that drew her to him and that made her toss out all her tried and true rules when it came to men. "Me," she whispered huskily.

"Exactly."

She knew what she wanted: King's Department Store to be saved, refurbished, expanded, to not just survive, but thrive. Recalling her stepmother's visit, she realized that to do the barracuda's bidding by marrying this man would also give Charlie what she wanted. But at what price?

Then she thought of Dolly, her friend and confidante. Deep down, she realized that her friend would forfeit this dream job if Charlie turned Alex down. Dolly had given up other opportunities in the past just to stay close to her. Didn't Dolly deserve a better life?

And she envisioned sales diving even lower and her friends being laid off. How could she do that to them?

In a flash, Charlie saw her own future stretch out in front of her. Long days at the office, struggling for changes at King's, battles with her stepmother each step of the way, countless meetings to sway the right people in the right places... It all seemed so bleak. So lonely.

Maybe all the fighting would still end with the same bleak results. Permanent closure of the store. It felt like another death to Charlie.

But if she accepted, then her stepmother guaranteed high profits for King's. That could only mean one thing to Charlie: Update the old and expand into other markets.

As she contemplated her answer, she could feel Alex's strong, steady gaze on her face. She was certain he read every mixed emotion that coursed through her body.

She peeked at him from under her lashes. A stranger. From the little she knew, he was all business, proper and stiff. Maybe if she got to know him, she'd be able to decide. Does he have any fun, she wondered.

"What's your favorite color?"

His eyes registered surprise, but the pat answer seemed to roll off his tongue. "Anything you're wearing."

She groaned. "That's cheesy."

"Cheesy?"

"And fake," she added. She rose and slowly wandered the room, trailing a hand over the back of the leather couch. She halted in front of the unlit fireplace.

\*\*\*

Alexander Royale gulped. Never in his life had he been remotely called fake before. Was it getting warm in here? "Turquoise."

Frowning, she cocked her head to the side as she stared at him. "Not green or blue? Turquoise?" she asked, sounding intrigued.

He hadn't opened up and revealed himself to any woman before. The cost had been too high. He'd shielded his heart for so long. Now he let out a shaky breath and prayed he was doing the right thing.

"Close your eyes and imagine," he said softly. He leaned his head back and closed his eyes. "It's quiet except for the gentle lap of water hitting the beach. Your bare toes curl in the warm, powdery white sand. A slight breeze caresses your body, lifting your hair, teasing it. The sun kisses your skin, stealing into every part of you, reaching out and heating all the cold spots deep, deep in your middle. You breathe in. The tang of salt hangs in the air and you can almost taste it on your lips. Ever so slowly you open your eyes. Before you is the most beautiful sight you've ever seen. Sun-sparkling water stretching for miles and miles, the color of—"

"Turquoise," they said it in unison.

He opened his eyes and couldn't mistake the dreamy look in hers.

She sighed. "Heavenly."

*No, you are.* "Yes, just like you'd imagine heaven would offer."

"Your island home." It wasn't a question.

He nodded. Had he exposed too much of himself? A tinge of heat crawled up the back of his neck.

Gazing at her, he realized gone was the guarded yet questioning stare. Her caramel-colored eyes seemed to sparkle.

The awkward tension seeped out of the atmosphere. Electricity crackled. His heart thudded in his chest. He dropped his gaze to her mouth. Oh, how he wanted to taste her lips.

She walked back to the chair and eased into it, facing him.

"So, Alex," she asked in a low, sexy voice, "are you a betting man?"

"I wouldn't be in the place I am today if I weren't."

"Professionally or personally?"

"Both." He liked the way her scent drifted to him, soft and feminine yet all Charlie.

She giggled. His heart jumped. "How did I know you were going to say that?"

Was she poking fun at him? He smiled, not caring.

"Got any cards around here?"

He stilled for a moment. Then, trying to keep a relaxed attitude, he waved to the small table between them. "In there. Why?"

"We'll let the cards decide our fate."

"New Age stuff?" He couldn't disguise the mixture of surprise and disappointment.

"No, silly."

No one had ever called him silly before either.

"I'll draw a card. High card wins. Aces high."

"Wins what?"

"You, of course."

He coughed a couple of times. "Me?"

"And you win me. High card, win, win. Marriage, eventually the baby carriage."

His chest tightened. "And if we don't win?"

"Poof! We go our separate ways. Me to restore King's back to the grand store it once was and you to your dinner parties, blind dates, and whatever else you do to find yourself a wife."

It sounded as dreadful as what he'd been through the last few months. Nodding toward the cards she now held, he said, "Go for it." In the back of his mind, he prayed.

Mesmerized, he watched her expertly shuffle the new deck. "You've done this before."

"Drawing for marriage, no way. Cards and Dolly on a Saturday night, definitely."

He chuckled at the image that sprang to his mind. Hopefully Dolly would come through for both of them.

Charlie handed him the deck. "Your turn."

At his quizzical look, she went on, "Hold them up facing you and fan them out."

Alex quickly completed the task, but he had a difficult time looking away from the vision of each card duplicated by the next. He refused to look over at her; he knew she'd see the truth in his eyes. Perspiration trickled down the back of his neck. Would she call him out?

Luckily for him, she reached over and plucked the middle card. She turned it around to read it.

"Ace of hearts," she murmured. "Go figure."

He swallowed hard again. Alex quickly folded the rest of the ace of hearts back into a deck and stuffed them in his shirt pocket, joining her silky nylons he'd tucked in there earlier.

"I win," he said, trying to block the elation from bubbling up inside of him.

"Correction, we win." Her conviction brought a wide smile to his lips and warmth through his middle.

"Yes, we do win." The knot of anxiety in his chest at duping her with the cards eased. He took a deep breath. "So I guess this means yes to my proposal." *Late, but still a yes.*

She winked. "You'll do."

He laughed outright at that.

She rose quickly, gathering her things.

He tensed. "Wait. Shouldn't we discuss details, rings, and all of that?" He stopped from ending with *and all that nonsense.*

"No ring." Her firm voice said it all.

"You're kidding me?" He'd never heard of such a thing.

"No engagement ring. I hate the competition and the flashy rocks. Wedding rings, yes. Plain. Simple. Meaningful."

She robbed him of speech. Never in his life had he met a woman who'd turn down a rock, as she so succinctly put it.

"The wedding. We'll keep it secret for now. Small, yet lovely. Private. Only family and a few close friends. And soon. Dolly and I will work it all out."

Was she always this decisive? He could get to like it very much.

When she remained silent, he asked with a grin in his voice, "Anything else I should know about?"

She crossed the room with long, confident strides. At the door, she turned fully to him, flashing a wide, easy smile that reached all the way to her sparkling eyes. Tingles swept through his body straight to his toes.

Tapping a finger on her lips as if in thought, she said, "Oh yes! You have to court me."

"Court you!" He couldn't disguise the shock reverberating through him.

She chuckled, opened the study door, and then turned back to him. "That's right. After the wedding." She closed the door behind her.

Stunned, all he could do was burst into laughter.

# CHAPTER 9

"She surprises me, Grandfather," Alex said as he stood at the floor-to-ceiling windows in his grandparents' library. "Every day, almost in every way. Imagine that." The last drifted away.

His gaze took in the scene outdoors. The small garden had been transformed into an impromptu wedding. Arches draped with flowers and vines, less than twenty white folding chairs circled nearby, and ribbons and flowers attached to the chairs outlined the aisle his bride would soon walk down. Tables waited in the distance, set with the finest linens, silverware, china, crystal stem ware, and with the finest food prepared by the top chefs. The few guests, in all their beautiful finery, arrived. Even from here he could hear the buzz of activity, the clinking of glasses, and delighted voices.

"Really, son? All women surprise me." His grandfather's gruff voice was soon followed by a few coughs.

Alex turned his back on the view. He frowned as the coughs came in fits and spurts. His grandfather, once so powerful and self-possessed, now seemed to have lost control of this battle with his health.

A prick of sadness pierced his chest. He owed everything to this man. Today, on his wedding day, he'd prove it, too. He could give his grandparents that much. He'd marry for them and soon produce the great-grandchild they longed for. He sighed inwardly.

Crossing the room, he took the armchair near the older man.

"Have I ever really thanked you, Grandfather?" He struggled with a well of emotion.

Grandfather, with his snowy-white hair and mustache to match, leaned his tall frame back. He smiled. "I'm not dying yet."

Alex winced and rubbed the back of his neck. "I didn't—"

The older man held up a hand. "No, no. Just teasing you." He sobered. "I've lost count of how many times you've thanked your grandmother and me over the years."

"If it weren't for you both…" He shuddered at the possibility of not being saved by them.

"We couldn't turn our backs on a boy who'd survived the plane crash his parents just died in."

Silence and sadness descended.

"But the way you did it. You could have sent me off to boarding school, checked in on weekends and holidays, paid the expenses and—"

"Not given a damn," his grandfather interrupted with a growl in his voice. "That never crossed our minds. Not once."

A smile tugged at Alex's lips. "No, Gramps, it wouldn't have." Admiration spread through his middle.

At Alex's use of his nickname, the older man's face relaxed and he beamed. "You're a fine young man."

"Not so young anymore," he corrected.

"You get to be my age and we'll talk, all right?"

"Yes, sir."

"I'm proud of you. Oh, not just for the things you do and get accomplished. It's how you treat people, how you go the extra mile. And why? Because, son, you care. You have a great heart."

Taken aback, Alex remained speechless. After a few silent moments, he choked out, "Thank you. You humble me. All my life I wanted to be like you, in business and in life. Now I think I'm getting there."

But was he? Something nudged Alex in the back of his mind. If his grandfather knew everything, would he still admire what Alex was doing to Charlie? Would Gramps think Alex had such a good heart then? Guilt pricked at him.

Alex had put getting married and having a child on the top of his agenda since his grandparents' health began to fade. Now he'd found the woman, never suspecting that he'd come to care for her in such a short time. To please his grandparents, he'd marry her today, but to keep his word with her stepmother, he was going to have to hurt Charlie.

Sometimes, he hated what he had to do. Would Charlie end up hating him, too?

\*\*\*

"Go on, shoo now, I tell you." Dolly shut the door behind her and let out an exasperated sigh.

Clutching her red cosmetics bag, Charlie crossed from the bathroom into the bedroom. "What was that all about?"

"That man of yours."

Surprised, Charlie stopped in her tracks. "What did Alex want?" Was he going to call off the wedding now that she'd warmed up to the idea? Her heart hitched.

Since the day she accepted his proposal, she'd been getting used to the idea of being a part of a real family again.

Dolly waved it off. "Oh, he just wants to talk to you, that's all."

"And that's not important?"

Her friend nabbed her by the arm and steered her to the dressing table. "It's bad luck to see the bride before the wedding, honey."

Charlie sank into the small chair. "We don't have to see each other to talk."

"Talk, see, same thing to me." She leaned around Charlie and picked up the hairbrush.

She glanced over at the phone. "I could call him."

"Nope. Don't be stirring up no bad luck now."

A loud knock sounded on the door.

"Now what?" Dolly asked, handing over the brush to Charlie. "If that's him again, I'm going to have to get tough this time."

Cringing, Charlie turned in her seat and leaned sideways to get a better look. Maybe she'd be able to shout something to him. Was he getting cold feet? A sliver of dread dropped into her middle.

"If I told you once, I told you twice you can't see her, got that, bub?" Dolly scolded as she whipped open the door. She stopped, frozen like a statue.

The silence was deafening.

"Dolly, what is it? Alex, is that you? Is something wrong?" Charlie rushed to the door.

"Well, I'll be a monkey's uncle," Dolly sputtered at the sight.

Reaching her friend, Charlie nearly lost her footing. "Francine. Priscilla." Her throat closed up.

Standing before her were visions of beauty. Gone were the usual black, dreary, and do-nothing-for-them dresses. The bridesmaids' gowns wore similar in fashion, yet Dolly had done wonders at sculpting the fabric ever so slightly here and there to bring out the girls' best features. "I, oh, I can't believe..." Only nonsensical things emerged from Charlie.

The sisters cried out in unison, "We're so beautiful, don't you think?"

Charlie nodded, dumbfounded. All speculation on Alex's request to see her flew out of her mind at the sight of her revamped sisters.

"And it's all thanks to you and Dolly." Francine twirled in the light blue satin gown Charlie had specifically designed to accentuate her small waist. The V neck hinted at the swell of bosom.

Priscilla, in pale green satin, brought them back to where they were. "Can we come in? We're here to help you get dressed."

They entered the room, closing the door behind them. Their uncharacteristic girlish giggles had Charlie glancing at Dolly. The older woman's wide-eyed stare had to mirror her own.

"Damn, we're good," Dolly said.

"Apparently so."

Charlie hooked her arm through Dolly's. They faced the remarkable change the make overs had wrought, not only in looks, but in their emerging bubbling personalities.

"Mother's cozying up to an elder gentleman downstairs, so we slipped on past her. Please don't let Mother see us until the wedding," Francine pleaded. "She'll have a hissy-fit and tell us to tie back our hair." She turned her head this way and that, the lush sweep of blonde hair swinging gently around her shoulders.

For the first time, Charlie noted the professional styled hairdos. Coming closer, she fingered Priscilla's silky strawberry blonde tresses. "How many inches did you get cut off?" Awe tinged her voice; she'd never seen the sisters in anything but one dreary style all their lives.

"Almost ten inches of hair, can you believe it? Francie only got eight cut off. But I just fell in love with this shorter bob. Don't you just love it?"

"Yes," Charlie said in all sincerity. "It does wonders for you."

Dolly chimed in, "Now, we just gotta get a little makeup on the three of you, and presto, the King sisters are transformed right before everyone's eyes. Imagine that."

The next half hour went by in a blur for Charlie. Between her and Dolly, and lots of fun and laughter, they skillfully applied the lightest of makeup on Francine and Priscilla, bringing out the warmth of their eyes and the who-would-have-ever guessed full lips and high cheekbones. Next, the trio had worked their magic on Charlie, making her hardly recognizable as the woman staring back at her when she finally slipped into her white satin wedding dress.

"Quit crying," Charlie chided. "You'll make me cry."

It didn't help. Dolly burst into tears. "Oh, you are the most beautiful bride I've ever seen. If only your momma and daddy could see you now."

Charlie bit her lip and blinked back the sting of tears at the mention of her parents. "He'd probably be swiping his forehead with his handkerchief right now as he tallied up the expenses for the wedding," she said with a well of fondness and a hint of a giggle in her voice.

The others chuckled.

"You ain't kidding, honey. Your daddy was an angel but the last few years he was alive, when it came to money, he'd count every penny." Dolly sniffed and then urged them to grab their bouquets.

Less than ten minutes later, Charlie made her way down the grand staircase and through the large, elegant home. "I have to go," she whispered to the three women assisting her down the garden stairs. She couldn't get a glimpse of Alex yet; he was at the altar farther in the garden, obscured by the lightly winding trail.

"No you don't. It's just nerves," Dolly chimed back.

"That's easy for you to say."

"Hah! I'm nervous for you. I could go, too, but we don't have the time."

"We'll go for you," Francine said, elbowing Priscilla. "Isn't that right?"

"How do women wear these things?" Priscilla asked, stumbling slightly.

"High heels, honey?" Dolly asked.

"No, thongs!" she said rather loudly.

There was a chorus of laughter from the nearby attendees.

"Oh, drat, I guess they heard me."

Before Charlie could respond, her stepmother appeared. "Stepmother." Her voice caught in the back of her throat. Instead of her usual black garb the barracuda had worn a dove gray gown. Charlie steeled herself as the woman's sharp eyes took in every detail.

"Hmmph!" she exclaimed at the sight of her two daughters. "We will have our talk after the ceremony. It wouldn't be right to spoil this occasion, now would it?"

The two sighs flew by Charlie as her sisters' tension eased.

"Now, Charlotte," her stepmother began. But she stopped herself and cleared her throat.

Charlie looked closer, getting a rare glimpse into the woman's dark eyes. She swore she saw moisture gathering there.

"You're a beautiful bride. Your father would be so very proud of you today, Charlotte." And with that, she nodded slightly and turned to be escorted down the small lane.

Shock rushed through Charlie. She couldn't ever recall her stepmother delivering a compliment without the backlash of a snide remark. And, to top it all off, she'd known exactly what to say about her father.

"Well, I'll be." Dolly whistled. "You think she's getting soft in her old age?"

A few minutes later, still feeling the recent hugs and kisses of Dolly and her sisters, Charlie made her way down the aisle. The wedding march played softly in the background as she rounded the bend. In the back of her mind, she recognized the ooh's and ahh's of the people she passed by; however, she held her breath until the moment she spotted Alex.

# CHAPTER 10

Charlie missed a step at the sight of him. Tall, dark-haired and handsome, he waited for her. His smile warmed her heart. His gaze captured hers. Her breath stilled. The tug of awareness pulsed through her. He wanted her. And she wanted him.

The stunning realization made her gasp. She wanted to marry him. Not for King's Department Store. For herself.

Coming to his side, she felt the tinge of warmth on her cheeks. Almost shy now, she said, "Hi." It came out in a breathy voice.

"Hi, yourself, beautiful." His mouth curved into a smile.

In a matter of minutes, she'd finally get to feel those lips on hers. Disconcerted, she said the first thing that popped into her head. "Do you come here often?"

His lips twitched. "As a matter of fact, I do."

Covering her mouth with a hand, she giggled. "Yes, I guess you do. After all, it's your grandparents' garden."

He chuckled along with her.

"Of course, you skinned your knees here as a boy, caught more than your share of frogs, and dug a few holes here and there."

"Ah, I see you've been talking to my grandmother. All that and I made a pest of myself," he added wistfully.

\*\*\*

Alex sobered as he took in every inch of her. He liked it when she wore her hair back and soft tendrils framed her beautiful face. Her bare shoulders revealed silky smooth skin he longed to touch. The dress, white and satin, molded to her exquisite curves and flared out near her ankles. Simple. Classic. Elegant. Just like Charlie.

A flash of color peeked out from under her hem, catching his attention. He looked closer. "The red shoes, Charlie?"

She giggled. "The one and the same pair. What is it with you and the shoes anyway?"

Smiling widely, he recalled the first time he'd met her. She crashed into him holding the strappy heels. He held her to him briefly, but a moment was all it had taken to want more of her. More warmth flooded him at the memory.

The minister interrupted his thoughts. "Are we ready to begin?"

"Yes," Charlotte said.

"No," Alex broke in.

"What?"

Gasps echoed all around him.

"Alex, my boy—"

"Just a minute, Gramps."

He turned to her and witnessed the crestfallen look on her face. She frowned. "But, I thought—"

"Wait. Before we do, I have to tell you something."

"Is this why you tried to see me earlier?" Worry gathered in her eyes.

"Yes."

She lowered her voice. "Don't you want to marry me?"

"Yes, but I have a confession to make."

More gasps, and louder this time, rang out.

He turned to the crowd, saying, "Not that!"

A few chuckles broke the tension.

"Alex, you're making me nervous. What is it?"

He swiped a hand over his brow. "It's the cards."

"Cards? Did he say cards?" Gramps nearly shouted.

"Yes, Gramps, I did." He pressed a hand over his eyes. Finally, he gave a sigh, dropped his hand, and then looked into her…laughing eyes? "Are you—?"

She nodded, beginning to giggle.

"The cards. All the same suit. All aces. You knew?" Wonder rushed through him, and then dawning struck.

"Blame Dolly," she choked out between fits of laughter.

He twisted around to look at the older woman fishing out a new deck of cards from her purse. "Works every time, Mr. R. Like a charm." She chuckled. "Hey, get it? Prince Charming, works like a charm."

Suddenly the garden rang with the sweet sound of hearty laughter.

"Remember, Alex, never bet against a sure thing," Charlie reminded him. "Not in ice cream—"

"Or cards. Or you." Alex stepped closer to Charlie, cupping her face in the palms of his hands. "Sweet Charlie, you knew all along."

"Not really. I figured it out along the way."

"If you didn't agree to marry me because of the bet, then why did you agree to marry me?"

"Turquoise," she whispered.

*All because of my favorite color?*

She stood on tip-toes and, ever so gently, brushed her lips against his. He sucked in a breath at the tender touch and the sweet taste of her.

"Hey, aren't you supposed to wait until you say your *I dos* first?" someone from the crowd called out.

Charlie broke the whisper-soft kiss, asking him, "Will you marry me, Alex?"

\*\*\*

The kiss. He'd never forget that kiss for as long as he lived.

Now, sitting on the floor in his study, he looked over at Charlie. He stared at her mouth as she ate a slice of pepperoni pizza. He dropped his gaze to the creamy satin nightwear and oh-so delicate matching lace-edged robe. Something tightened in his middle. He glanced away. "So what do we do now?" he muttered under his breath.

"It's our wedding night. What do you think people do?"

Alex turned sharply, holding his breath. He knew what he'd like to do.

"Get to know each other, of course."

He sighed. "Of course."

She giggled. He smiled.

"I'm sorry to disappoint you, Alex, but I'm not that kind of girl."

He shook his head and suppressed a wider smile. "I never thought you were." He stopped to gather his thoughts. Leaning back against a nearby chair, he stretched out his jean clad legs, crossing them at the ankle and laced his fingers behind his head. "So, tell me about yourself, Mrs. Royale."

Charlie sucked in a breath and then tried to swallow a few times. She gingerly placed the unfinished slice of pizza back in the box.

Eyeing her, he said, "That's right, you are Charlotte Royale, now."

"Charlotte *King* Royale," she corrected in a strained voice. She blinked. Clearing her throat, she said, "I'll always be a King, Alex."

He noticed moisture gather in her eyes. His heart tugged. He lowered his arm, and then dragged a hand over his eyes. "I know. No one can ever take that away from you or where you came from." He trailed off, wondering what in the world he was doing, trying to rob her of her late father's business.

Her light, brief touch on his forearm had him jerking back to the moment. "Thank you," she barely whispered, making him almost wish he'd told her about King's Department Store. Almost.

If a person was capable of mentally kicking himself, he'd just done it.

"You first," she said.

"Huh? Did I miss something?" The way she jumped from one subject to another astounded him at times.

"Tell me about yourself, silly."

Tipping his hand, he said, "I know I'm not that interesting, so ladies first."

She wagged a finger at him. "Oh, so that's how you are."

Warmth spread along his cheeks. "Duly chastised."

Before he had a chance to do anything, she'd leaned over and pecked him on the cheek. By the time he'd realized what she'd done, she was reseated. He chuckled. "You, my dear, are very quick."

"Can't keep up?"

The challenge in her tone brought heat to his body. "Loaded question," he muttered.

"For shame, Alex."

At that he threw back his head and laughed.

"All right, if you must know, I love pepperoni pizza."

He moved so now his arm rested on his bent knee as he faced her. "Oh, really." He nodded as she scooped up the piece she'd recently discarded. "I'd never have guessed. Champagne? Caviar? Strawberries and whipped cream? Having an intimate wedding dinner with flowers and candlelight? Nah. She wants to eat delivered pizza while sitting on the floor."

She giggled, taking another bite. Her soft moans of appreciation shot through him. Once she'd chewed and swallowed, she pointed out, "You forgot the cozy fire in the fireplace."

Alex grinned. "That makes all the difference."

Looking at him sheepishly, she confessed, "I'm not terribly romantic."

"No, I can't say that about you, especially after your reaction to my proposal."

She reached over and put a hand over his mouth. "Quit!"

He grabbed her hand, nibbling on her fingers. "Yummy, pizza."

Tugging her hand away, she snatched up a napkin. "You are never going to let me live that down, are you?"

Glee shot through him. "No. I'm going to enjoy retelling that story over and over again to our kids and their kids." He noted the way her eyes darkened.

"Kids?"

This time he was the one who swallowed hard. "Yes."

"How many?"

"As many as you want." He heard the husky timber in his own voice as he thought about making love to her. "At least one," he added.

"I…" She stopped. Slowly, she put aside the half eaten slice. Wiping her mouth and hands, she refused to look directly at him. "I have a confession to make."

Something hit him in the gut. "Confession? Now?" *Please don't let her say it was a mistake. Please don't let her say she doesn't want kids.*

She looked at him under her lashes and the knot of desire twisted in him.

"I never imagined that I would ever be a wife, never mind a mother." She held up a hand. "Wait, let me explain. Since my father died, King's Department Store is all I've ever dreamt about. Making it a success has driven me for years. For all intents and purposes, I'm a workaholic." She shrugged her shoulders. "This is all new to me, Alex."

He slowly released his pent-up breath. "Me, too. I mean I've worked hard all this time. Getting married was the last thing I ever thought about."

"Until your grandparents became ill."

"Yes."

"But you waited."

"For the right one."

"Me?"

"Yes, Charlie, for you."

He heard her swift intake of breath. "What's so special about me?"

For the first time he could recall, he spoke without thinking. "The question is more like, what isn't special about you?"

\*\*\*

In awe, Charlotte King Royale watched her husband. He had a way about him that drew her to him.

He'd finally opened up more than an hour ago. But it had been his question about what wasn't special about her that had allowed her to see beyond the image of the man she'd just married. She'd pictured him as stiff, proper, and business-like, but he'd let down that guard and hinted at more than just a mere physical attraction to her. She hadn't been the lesser of all evils when it came to choosing a wife.

Admiration shone in his eyes.

Hope filled her heart.

Now she watched the way his eyes lit up and the way his smile came easily as he told her another story about growing up. His voice, deep and husky, poured over her like rich honey. He moved his hands to describe yet another adventure and she took in every detail of his large palms and long fingers. What would those hands feel like on her? An ache deep inside her pulsed.

She longed to lean over and brush back his hair and trace the contours of his face. Then she wished she could taste his firm mouth. Softly at first, and then deeply. She shivered.

"Are you listening?" he asked with a smile in his voice.

"Yes, go on. I can't wait to hear how you explained it all away to your grandmother."

He chuckled. "It wasn't easy. Looking back now, I'm sure I saw her lips twitch more than once. But," he shrugged, "who wouldn't want to laugh at how an eight-year-old boy could nearly destroy her entire china set?"

"By using them as Frisbees—"

"To feed the birds peanut butter and jelly sandwiches."

She joined him in laughter as the vision took hold.

Moments later, his smile lingered and he sighed. Her heart hitched.

What was it about him, like no other man, that tugged at her?

# CHAPTER 11

Hours later, Alex halted at her bedroom door.

"Thank you for a lovely evening." Her soft voice tickled him in the semi-darkness of the hallway.

Only a few inches separated them. He inhaled deeply, savoring her tantalizing scent. Part Charlie, part flowers. Where did her fragrance end and the perfume begin? He wished he could discover that secret tonight. "Thank you for marrying me." He meant it.

"So what do we do now?" she whispered.

Something tugged deep and low inside him. "A goodnight kiss?"

"You have the most brilliant ideas, Alex."

"That's why you married me," he said.

"One of many reasons."

He wondered what the other reasons were. Maybe someday she'd tell him.

"Are you going to kiss me?"

He chuckled. He brushed back a lock of her hair and cupped her face in his hands. "It would be my pleasure."

Her eyes fluttered shut and her lips parted. He groaned softly. Alex lowered his head. Ever so gently, he teased her with a whisper of a kiss. This time she was the one to groan. Desire curled in his middle.

Alex deepened the kiss, parting her sweet, tender lips with his tongue. Hunger swept through his blood at her ready response.

In mid-kiss, he felt her hands at his waist, her fingers skimming the fabric of his shirt. The warmth of her skin burned through the thin barrier. Flames of liquid heat licked at him, urging him on.

But he held himself in check.

Moments later, he sensed her reluctance as he ended the embrace. Her shivery sigh-part pleasure, part disappointment- matched his increasing regret. Why in the world did he agree to wait? And what did she mean by courting her? She'd made it clear she wasn't the least bit romantic.

Slowly, he stepped away, releasing her. He stuffed his hands in the pockets of his jeans. "Well, I guess this means goodnight."

She bit her bottom lip. He watched with a mixture of lust and fascination. He dragged his gaze away from the tantalizing image.

He leaned forward and tenderly kissed her on her forehead. "Goodnight, Charlie."

"Sweet dreams, Alex."

Walking away, he sensed her stare. Alex willed himself to keep on going down the hallway and not turn back. A few steps more and he was at his door. Reaching out, he grasped the doorknob. He stilled for a moment. Clenching his teeth, he fought his conscience. Honor won.

Once in his room, Alex plopped down on the edge of his bed. He dropped his head into his hands. Berating himself for wanting what he couldn't have, he nearly missed the soft tap at his door. He sucked in a breath.

He opened the door slowly. "Charlie?" *Don't tempt me any more than I already am.*

She wrung her hands. "I was wondering, is it important to you, well, if someone gives you their word, would you expect them to keep it?"

He blinked a few times, frowning. "Yes."

A heavy sigh rushed out of her. "I thought so. Goodnight."

Alex shook his head. Gently, he closed the door. "Shower. Long. Cold. Now." He tugged at the buttons on his shirt, undoing them swiftly. Just as he went to shrug it off, a hesitant knock came again. He froze. "No, please no."

The sound seemed to resound in his head.

Gritting his teeth, he felt the muscle throbbing along his jaw. Alex answered the door.

This time her hands were folded together, fingers linked together as if in some sort of prayer. "I hate to bother you."

"No bother," he lied, smiling tightly.

Her gaze seemed to linger on the opening of his shirt. He inhaled sharply.

Charlie went on, "You know the question I just asked you? Well, I've got another one, sorta related." She winced slightly. "Would you think less of someone if they gave their word, but changed their minds?"

He contemplated that for a short time. "Probably. Yes, I guess I would. Your word is your honor. Why?"

She waved a hand at him. "Oh, just asking."

He watched her turn on her heel and walk away. He closed the door with a definite snap. Turning, he whipped off his shirt, flinging it on the bed. Making his way into the bathroom, he undid the snap and zipper on his jeans.

A knock, loud and strong, rent the air.

He groaned. "You have got to be kidding me." Alex clenched his fists and clamped his eyes shut. "Go away, please, just go away."

It came again, more confident than the last.

Alex marched to the door and then threw it open. "Charlie, I am not a saint, got it?"

In the next instant, she rushed to him, wrapping her arms around his neck and kissing him. All he could do was hold her. Stilling, she pulled away. "Alex, kiss me back."

"I can't. If I do, I won't be able to stop."

"I don't want you to stop," she said. Her eyes seemed to gather with moisture. "Alex, I'm sorry, but I'm taking my word back."

"Your word?"

"Yes, you don't have to court me first. You can do that later."

Shock raced through him. He pulled back from her, searching her stare. "Are you sure, really sure about this?"

There was no hint of reluctance.

"I've never been more sure about anything in my life."

\*\*\*

Charlie could never pinpoint the exact moment she'd changed her mind. Maybe it had been somewhere between the wedding confession about the cards or simply talking to him late into the night over pizza and soda. She just knew the moment he ever so gently kissed her on the forehead and walked away that she longed for him. Deeply, achingly longed for Alexander Royale.

The physical appeal had been obvious even when she'd seen his picture in the papers. But, for every moment she'd spent with him, discovered a little bit more about him, she'd been slowly and steadily yearning for the man. Honor. Integrity. Compassion.

Now, with dawn streaking the sky outside, she snuggled into him. Her head rested on his shoulder and his arms wrapped around her. She sighed with contentment.

"Charlie," he murmured, trailing his fingers along her bare arm.

She shivered. "Hmmmm?"

"Thank you."

"For what?" she whispered.

"For taking your word back."

She giggled. Moving so she faced him, she said softly, "My pleasure, husband." She leaned down and brushed her lips against his. His groan rumbled through his chest, making heat coil within her. "But, remember, you still have to court me."

He chuckled heartily, and then grabbed her in his arms and rolled her to her back. Charlie ran her hands over his biceps and to his shoulders.

Looking down at her, he said, "I think I can do that." He trailed kisses along her jaw and down her neck. He nibbled at the sensitive spot at the base of her throat. "Like this?"

She sucked in a sharp breath. "Hmmm, yes. That's a perfect place to begin with. Right there, Alex. Court away."

# CHAPTER 12

Charlie hummed as she draped the lush, ruby red fabric trimmed in gold over the back of the ornamental chair in the display window.

She felt the nudge on her arm.

"You're mighty happy, honey," Dolly pointed out, plumping up a matching pillow on the opposite chair. "I wonder why."

"Dolly!" Charlie's cheeks warmed instantly. She straightened, rubbing the small of her back. "I can't go into details of my wedding night, even to you."

The older woman winked and nodded her head. "I gotcha. Edward and I were betting on you and Mr. R.," she cleared her throat, "gettin' to know each other, close like."

Her cheeks burned now. She plopped down in the chair and dropped her face into her hands. "This is so embarrassing. You and Edward betting on that!" A new thought had her snapping her head up and twisting to see Dolly settling back in the matching gold chair. "You didn't hear anything, did you?"

Dolly slapped her hand on her thigh. "No such luck." She leaned close and whispered loudly, "'Cause me and Edward snuggled a little bit."

"No way!"

"Way!"

"Why you, you—"

"Hussy?" Dolly giggled and her face turned pink. She shrugged self-consciously. "I can't help myself around that man. What a hunk!"

Charlie cupped a hand over her mouth and chuckled.

Her friend tapped her on the arm. "He's a great kisser. Oh my, the things he does!"

"Stop!" She covered her ears. "Don't tell me. I'll never be able to look at him again if you do."

"And his hands," she practically growled, "nice and firm, but not too strong, if you know what I mean."

Charlie had visions of Alex running his palms over her skin. She shivered uncontrollably. "Quit," she groaned.

"Why? You gonna rush home or something?" Dolly raised and lowered her brows.

"Something like that," Charlie confessed. She eased all the way back in the chair and, with her foot, dragged the ottoman over. She and Dolly rested their feet on the footstool at the same time.

"That good, huh?"

"Better."

They giggled.

"I guess all them stories 'bout him were true then."

"Yep." She smiled. An ache throbbed to life somewhere deep and low. Charlie sighed.

There was a moment of silence as Charlie watched beyond the glass window and noted the usual slow, steady stream of Sunday foot traffic on the street. No one took notice of her and her friend redecorating one of King's Department store windows. That seemed to be a problem. No one noticed because fewer and fewer people shopped at King's.

"Hey," Dolly said, dragging Charlie back to the moment, "you think Edward and Mr. R. talk about these kinda things?"

"Compare notes?"

"Yeah. I wonder what they say."

"That we're good, of course."

Dolly burst out laughing. Charlie soon joined her.

A few minutes later, Charlie asked, "Do you think this will work, Dolly? I mean," she waved a hand at the bogus deck of cards on the table between them, the mannequins eerily similar to her and Alex nearby waiting to be gently positioned in the chairs they occupied, "all this?" As she glanced over her shoulder at the bold-faced family name she'd contrived, she winced. "The Charmings?"

Her friend must have heard the nervous edge in her voice; she said, "Honey, all these people have been wondering about you and Mr. R. The papers, the reporters, the questions, all the juicy details. This is the perfect way to let them in on what's going on. And get a whole lotta interest back in King's."

She bit her lip. Recalling the other display window they'd just finished nearly an hour ago, Charlie wondered what Alex's reaction would be to an image of him proposing to her on the impression of the yacht she and Dolly had created.

Dolly tapped a finger on the deck of cards nestled on the table between them. "The first window's a teaser. People are going to see that and rush to this one. Won't they get a good chuckle over your engagement and the fake cards?"

She tried to smile, she really did, but a muscle near her lip twitched instead.

The idea for the displays had come to her as she showered that morning. Still dripping wet, she'd hurried to her sketch pad and, with a few quick strokes, had both drawings coming to life right before her very eyes. She'd had her friend involved shortly thereafter as they dreamed up fabrics and colors. Charlie had thought nothing of getting approval from her husband. He'd departed the house nearly an hour before.

Now, she realized she didn't have license to broadcast his life. "But Alex?"

Dolly waved her off. "Oh, pooh! That man has had everyone and their brother dissecting him for years. He's used to it. And why can't his wife and her store get a little cashola from it? You know how much business this is going to drum up, honey?"

She imagined the revival of King's and the increase in sales, especially among the younger female demographics. "Who wouldn't want to buy into the fantasy of love, right?"

"Righto!"

Almost a half hour later, Charlie rearranged her mannequin, the last piece put into place. Stepping back, she tapped a finger to her lips. Then she snapped her fingers. "Ah hah! That's it. She's got the wrong shoes on. No one is going to buy yesterday's pumps. I've got just the perfect pair in my office. Dolly, wait here, I'll be back in a jiffy."

"But-"

"Gotta rush," she called back as she dashed through the unlit, empty store and to the elevator. In her stocking feet, she slid across the marble floor. She giggled, recalling how every Sunday when the store was closed, her father and she would kick off their shoes and compete on who could slide the farthest. Time and time again, he'd let her win.

She sighed at the heart-tugging memories as the doors silently closed and she rode up in the gold-mirrored compartment. Charlie closed her eyes and rubbed the back of her neck as more thoughts crowded her mind. She had to save this store for her father. He poured his heart and soul into every last detail, always putting the customer first on his list.

He'd often said, "Never forget, Charlie, people deserve to be treated with the utmost care. We at King's are here to serve them. It's a privilege. They work hard for their money and nothing but the best is good enough for them. Everyone's included, from the man who digs ditches for a living to the richest woman in the world. We treat everyone with respect, kindness, and compassion."

As the bell dinged and the doors whispered open, Charlie blinked back tears.

Her father knew what he'd been talking about. For a man who'd begun life with nothing, watching his parents toil away picking up garbage and cleaning houses, he'd never forgotten what it had been like to have others look down on him. Never had he done it to anyone else. Nor would Charlie.

Distracted, she made her way into King's corporate offices and headed to hers. She thought she heard voices from the opposite direction. Her stepmother's office? She shook her head, knowing her stepmother never worked on Sundays. The sound came again. Two distinct voices.

Charlie stilled. Slowly, she turned on her heel. With ever-increasing dread, she made her way past the vacant receptionist desk, the closed doors lining the way, and down the long, plush carpeted hallway. The double doors beyond her stepmother's assistant's desk stood open.

A tall male figure, with his back to her, came into view. Broad shouldered, dark hair, and rich deep voice, he evoked a deep tug of recognition. She nearly tripped.

What was he doing here with her stepmother? Her middle dipped.

Her stepmother, standing behind her desk, wore her customary black suit and pinched-lipped expression. "Really?"

"Yes, really, Mrs. King."

"I won't stand for this."

"You're the one trying to renege. More money?"

"Additional fees."

Entering the room, Charlie remained unnoticed. She gulped.

"I'll tell the press. First, I'll tell Charlie."

"She won't believe you," he baited.

"Believe what, Alex?" she asked, trying to keep the hurt from her voice. She failed miserably.

He turned quickly to her. For a moment, she glimpsed the shock in his eyes and the color drain from his face. But he recovered quickly. Soon he flashed a hesitant smile and jammed his hands in his pockets. "Charlie, what are you doing here?"

"Charlotte King," her stepmother admonished, "how dare you sneak up on people. I'll have you know this is a private conversation."

For once, she didn't counter with a funny comeback. Staring directly at her husband, she asked the questions tumbling through her mind. "Alex, what's going on?

Why would you be talking to my stepmother, of all people, on the day after our wedding? And what exactly won't I believe?"

She watched him closely. He swallowed hard. Something clouded his eyes. "I can't tell you."

His softly delivered answer only fueled her curiosity more. Frowning, she turned to the woman stepping from behind the large desk, straightening her suit jacket. Dread pooled in Charlie's middle. "Stepmother, what in the world is going on?"

Her stepmother raised a hand to smooth her always perfect hair into place. "Well, if you must know, I'll tell you—"

"No," Alex cut in.

The older woman sighed heavily. "More's the pity about the additional fees." She shrugged a shoulder. "She's going to find out sooner or later." Turning her full attention back to Charlie, she said, "I'm leaving King's."

Charlie jerked her head back. Never had she imagined her stepmother would resort to this. "Quitting?" Her mind raced with thoughts. "Who will replace you as president? Me?" Hope and anxiety balled together in her chest.

The woman before her inhaled sharply and raised her chin. "I am not a quitter. No, Charlotte, I've sold King's to your husband."

Shock reverberated through her body. Blood rushed in her ears. "What!? But, it's my family's store."

"You, my dear, are not cut out to be in charge of King's," the woman said coldly. "I've told you that for years. Maybe you'll listen now."

Shaking her head, she looked at Alex. "No, you can't."

"I'm sorry, I did."

She brushed aside the deep well of sadness coloring his voice. Then dawning struck. "You," she pointed at him, and then at her stepmother, "you planned this, didn't you? Together."

He reached out for her. "Charlie, let me explain."

Drawing farther away, she said, "No, don't touch me."

"Oh really, Charlotte, must you be so dramatic?" the older woman scolded. "Of course we planned this. How else do you think I agreed to this marriage? You know your father gave me the final say in your choice of a husband. If Alexander hadn't have said he'd buy the store, he'd never have the chance to marry you." She could have ended with "silly girl" for the tone of her voice.

An invisible dagger pierced her heart. "Alex, how could you be a part of destroying my dream? How could you?"

Who was this man she'd married?

\*\*\*

In a million years he'd never be able to explain it to her, Alex thought with a heavy weight sitting in his chest. Hell, he couldn't even explain it to himself.

Thinking she was close to fainting, he'd helped her out of the office and found Dolly, carrying Charlie's shoes, near the receptionist's counter. The older woman had grown alarmed at the sight of Charlie and soon had them all bustling in the car. She'd ordered Edward to whisk them back home again.

Now, Charlie sat on one side of the car, staring out the window, while he sat on the opposite side doing the same. In the front seat he heard Dolly ask his driver, "What happened, Eddie?"

"I don't know." Edward seemed as puzzled as she did. Maybe even as much as Alex was at the rapid decline of his own marriage.

Alex felt the quick stare of Edward in the rearview mirror. He shook his head sadly, but didn't bother to look directly at his friend.

"When Miss Charlie didn't come back to the display window right away, I rushed off after her. Don't you know the barracuda was there and," she pointed her thumb to Alex in the back seat, "he was there talking to the old battle-ax."

Edward groaned.

"You do know something."

"Not everything," he defended.

"For Pete's sake, they're in cahoots, aren't they? Why else would he need to go talk to her *after* the wedding?"

His friend remained silent.

The strain stretched awkwardly. "Miss Charlie is fighting back tears and you don't have the decency to tell me what's going on?"

Turning his head to her for a brief moment, Edward said, "Well, he's not doing much better either. And he's the one paying me."

"We can hear you two," Charlie said matter-of-factly, still looking out the window. "And, Dolly, he pays your salary, too."

The older woman made a dismissive noise in the back of her throat. "I can get a job like that." She snapped her fingers. "I only took it because of you marrying him. So we could be together again. But, I can leave him and anyone else," she emphasized, leaning slightly toward Edward, "anytime. Believe you me." She sat back in her seat and with her chin set at a stubborn angle, she stared straight ahead. "Men!"

"Women," Edward muttered.

Alex groaned silently. How in the world was he going to fix the mess he'd made of everything?

# CHAPTER 13

In the entrance of his home, Alex called out to his wife as she headed toward the stairs, "Charlie, we need to talk."

She halted. Slowly, she pivoted to him. Her eyes were filled with sadness. "Don't you think we should have done that before yesterday?"

"I couldn't take the chance." There, he'd been honest.

"Chance at what?" Dolly asked, lingering in the foyer.

"This is private," Edward chastised her.

"Private, smivate, Eddie. Anything that happens to Miss Charlie is my business."

Alex nearly groaned. This was not going to be the easiest conversation he'd ever had, especially with an audience. "Charlie, I'm sorry. I never meant to hurt you."

She inhaled sharply and jerked her head back slightly. "No, Alex, I truly don't think you meant to hurt me. That's because you weren't thinking of me at all. How could you be so selfish as to agree to her terms?"

"What terms, honey?" Dolly asked abruptly.

Charlie glanced at her friend. "The barracuda sold me to the highest bidder."

"Sold?!" Dolly, Alex, and Edward cried out at the same time.

"Yes, sold." Charlie looked to all of them. Finally, she settled her stare on Alex. "What else would you call it? You, my husband, gets a wife, but, in return, you must purchase the family business."

"King's! She sold him King's?" Dolly's horrified question ripped through the group.

He sighed heavily, pushing back his suit jacket and resting his fists on his hips. Between clenched teeth, he pointed out, "And tell me, wife, would I have bought the damn place if she'd offered up Francine or Priscilla? No," he answered his own question. "I wanted you." He still wanted her, with an ache so deep and so wide he had no idea if he'd ever get his fill of her.

For a moment, she seemed stunned as she shook her head and blinked a few times. "You could have anyone. The papers had you linked to high-society women for years. Stunning, elegant, well-mannered." Her confusion colored her words. "Any one of them would have been more than appropriate. You could have handpicked your wife."

"I did."

That had her stepping back and grasping ahold of the banister. She frowned. "Not for King's?"

He blew out a hot breath. "No, Charlie, not for King's. It's more trouble than anything else. It's losing money and Royale Enterprises will be strained just trying to take it over." He didn't dare tell her just how much of a burden her family store would be to his family's business. And he still had to justify it to Grandfather. How, he had no clue.

All he'd known from the first night he'd met her is that he wanted her, the beautiful, exuberant, smart, funny sparkling woman. And at any price. Looking at her now, he suddenly realized he'd paid the ultimate price. With his heart.

He loved her.

The knowledge slashed through him like lightning, zapping his nerves and shocking his mind even more. "Son- of-a—" he muttered, staring at her in awe.

"I can fix that," Charlie pleaded.

"What?" *My heart?*

"The profits. I have so many wonderful ideas for the store. I even came up with a new concept this morning."

Dolly piped in, "Oh, Mr. R., she's got pages after pages of notes and sketches. Why, the barracuda brushed her off for years, never wanting to update anything." She snorted. "She probably didn't want to part with any of that cold, hard cash. Greedy woman!"

For once Dolly was being kind about the woman. Alex rubbed the back of his neck. He'd figured he had to spruce it up a bit to resell the place. But, he knew that's not what Charlie had in mind at all.

"Sir," Edward interrupted his thoughts. "It doesn't seem feasible."

He noted his friend's wrinkled brow, knowing Edward was privy to many of the goings-on.

He sighed heavily. "No, it doesn't."

Charlie stepped near. "Alex, give me a chance, will you? I can make a difference."

Passion and desperation glowed in her look. Admiration shot through him. He loved the fight in her, the drive, the determination, and so much more.

He recalled her stepmother's cutting remark about Charlie never being leadership material. Charlie had wanted that opportunity and her stepmother had blocked her at every turn.

Could he allow this? If he did, how much harm could it do? As long as he didn't promise her he'd keep the store.

He even said as much. "Charlie, I can't promise the store won't be sold after all."

He watched her swallow hard. "I'll take the risk. What more will I have to lose than what I'll lose now if I do nothing?"

Hope. Faith, he thought wistfully.

And, when all was said and done, would she end up hating him for it? What if he lost her, too?

Closing his eyes, he sensed the three of them staring long and hard, waiting for his answer. He rubbed a hand over his face, and then looked at his wife. "All right."

"Yippee," she shouted and Dolly soon joined in. Charlie threw her arms around him and hugged him tight. "Thank you, thank you, thank you. You won't be sorry."

Holding her in his arms, he couldn't seem to get enough of her warmth and special scent. He prayed she wouldn't be sorry once the end came to the store.

"This is so exciting," she said, giving him a quick kiss on his cheek and then pulling away.

The imprint of her lips lingered on his flesh and he longed to draw her back for more. But he didn't. As he watched his wife's glee while hugging Dolly, he knew he'd done the right thing. For now. Glancing over at Edward, his middle sank at the look of doubt. The little bit of anxiety gnawed at his gut.

"Conditions," Edward mouthed to him. He nodded his head in Charlie's direction.

Alex cleared his throat. "Yes, there has to be some conditions, of course."

Charlie, beaming, turned back to him. "Of course, how silly. Yes—"

"Wait," Dolly interrupted. "We've got to discuss a few things first." She whispered in Charlie's ear. Charlie responded in the same manner.

Unfortunately, Alex couldn't hear a darn word either woman said. Frowning, he looked at his friend. They seemed to shrug in unison. *Beats us.*

Once the women were done, they linked arms, turning to Alex. "Our first condition is our marriage remains a secret, well, to the public mostly," Charlie amended the last.

"Secret?" Puzzled, he couldn't fathom how that would affect King's in the least. If anything, it might draw in more curious shoppers.

"Yes, until I'm," her friend jabbed her in the ribs, "we're comfortable with the announcement."

He dragged a hand through his hair. "Just how are we supposed to keep this under wraps?"

"We have so far. We haven't been seen in public together, for the most part. No one but the family and a few friends know about the ceremony and none of the papers have asked questions about any nuptials. I think we've done a darn good job."

Alex blew out a hot breath. "All right. What's the second condition?"

"You put me in charge of King's."

This time the request didn't come out as bold or confident.

He nearly bit his tongue to keep the question from popping out of his mouth. Was she certain she could handle the pressure? But he refrained, not wishing to hurt her.

She'd already had too many duties at the store. With taking over the top spot, she'd be stretched to the limit and then some.

"And remain art director?"

"Yes."

If he put a time limit on this maybe-just maybe-it wouldn't be too overwhelming for her. Fat chance. But could he completely snatch her dream away from her? This would surely be her one and only chance to fulfill that desire. Who was he to rob her of that, too?

"Agreed." He held up his hand as she and Dolly clapped their hands. "But you have four weeks to do it in."

"Eight," she bargained.

"Five."

"Six and we have a deal."

He chuckled. Holding out his hand, he said, "Deal."

She disentangled herself from her friend and placed her hand in his. Small, soft, yet firm and strong. His wife was a mixture of contradictions. And he loved that about her.

Raising an eyebrow, he asked, "Kiss?"

Before he knew what was happening, she brushed her lips against his. She giggled as she raced up the stairs with Dolly behind her. Charlie called out, "But you've still got to court me. Six weeks should do."

# CHAPTER 14

With neat piles of paper stacked carefully on her desk, Charlie snatched up the ringing phone. "Did you get him?"

Her assistant's chirpy voice sang back, "I'm the girl wonder, whatcha think? He's on line one."

"Thanks, Peg, ol' great one." She smiled as she punched the one on her phone. "Rico, I can't thank you enough for returning my call."

"Sweetie, anything for you."

"I'm glad you feel that way, because I have an offer for you."

"Ohhhhhh! Who is he and what does he look like?"

"Quit! It's not a date." She heard him mutter in her ear. "Sorry, friend, I'm no matchmaker. But I can get you one of the hottest jobs in town."

"Really?" His voice piqued with interest. "Do tell."

"With me."

"You? Oh, honey, are you finally kicking that place to the curb and starting your own design biz?"

She laughed then. "Not quite. I am taking over, though."

"No way!"

"Way!"

"Details, details!"

Well, she couldn't tell all, but she did fill him in about her new position. She ended with, "And there are going to be lots of changes over the next few weeks. Remember when we talked about you and your team taking over the salon here at King's for a week, performing makeovers on our customers?"

"That was ages ago and the barracuda turned us down flat."

"She doesn't have a say-so now. I do."

He whistled softly. "Oh, I love make overs. Publicity? Before and after shots? Clothes, makeup, hair, undies, everything?"

"The works."

"Count me in, honey."

After hanging up on the third similar call, Charlie eased back in her chair. "Yes, yes, yes!" Things were working out just fine.

She'd arranged for one of her friends at an advertising firm to assist in the marketing. And, to top it all off, she'd gotten the best-known print ad photographer to not only take the before and after pictures for the makeovers, but to snap shots for a special advertising campaign she dubbed Operation Charmings. Starring her, of all people.

She mulled over her predicaments. Two, she knew of. First, Dexter. Would he be so willing to help her? She'd hurt him. Not on purpose, but nonetheless she had. She sighed heavily. Not once had she led him on. His brilliance and ideas had sparked a kinship.

But romance? No. Well, not on her part. Obviously, it had on his.

Brushing that dilemma aside for now, she focused on the next one. Alex. His actions stunned her. Making a deal with the barracuda. Buying the store to marry her. Now he wanted to destroy the one thing that she'd dreamt of for so long. How could he?

She quickly reminded herself it wasn't her personally he wanted to harm. No, if she believed him, he'd gone to great measures just to get her stepmother's approval to marry her. At first it seemed difficult to grasp.

But he'd pled his case and made it plausible. He'd have never done it for her stepsisters. No, he'd have walked away and not had a second thought or a lingering doubt.

But for her, he'd bargained.

"With a master, at that," she muttered, thinking of how shrewd and calculating her stepmother could be most of the time.

"Why me?" she wondered aloud.

"Why not, honey?" Dolly asked as she stood with her hands on her hips and filling the doorframe.

Surprised, Charlie sat upright. "Dolly? When did you get here?"

"Just in time, by the looks of it." The older woman waved a hand at her. "Come on, the unveiling is about to take place."

She glanced at the clock on her phone, and then jumped up. "Already?"

Not quite nine in the morning, Charlie and Dolly rushed to the display windows. A crowd of employees gathered at the entrance, waiting for the curtains to drop and the secretive display windows to be revealed.

"Oh, I almost forgot to tell you the piece d' resistance," Dolly said, huffing the last few yards.

"More surprises?"

"Yep. I called Edward to fill him in. He's bringing Mr. R."

Charlie stopped in her tracks. "What?!" It was one thing to create this story of the Charmings, but quite another to have to come face to face with one of the "characters" who didn't even know he was in the darn story to begin with.

"Righto! He's out there now. We'll watch from outside, too. And with the press. They came just like you said they would after you made the calls. Peg's gonna pull the drape for each one."

"But." Charlie's nerves bubbled in her middle. "The shoes." She pointed past Dolly. "I've got to—"

"Done."

"Done. How?"

"I did it just like you asked me to this morning, don't you remember?"

The air rushed out of her. That was nearly three hours and lots of work ago. "Oh." She struggled for another thought. "You know Peg can't do both drapes. It would be too much for her to rush from one to the next. I'll do it myself." What better way to face her husband's reaction than by having a thick pane of glass between them?

Before Dolly could stop her, Charlie made her way around several employees as they offered well wishes. She absently greeted them with a smile pasted on her face. The air buzzed with excitement. Word had traveled fast. The barracuda was out and Charlie was in charge, making sweeping changes for the better.

"Honey!"

For once in her life, Charlie ignored Dolly's call. Time seemed to stop as she slowly made her way up the short number of stairs. Peg, six foot and model thin, fidgeted with the gold-tasseled cord.

"I'll take this one," Charlie said.

She frowned. "Holy Saint Nick, are you sure?"

One of the few people to know about the secret romance and attended the private wedding, Peg sensed there could be consequences. She'd said as much earlier when Charlie filled her in on her plans.

"You know he's here."

Charlie swallowed hard. "I heard."

"It could get sticky."

"Why do you think I'd rather be here than there?"

Peg chuckled. "I would, too." She winced. "Sorry, boss, but for a guy who's had his whole life on display, no pun intended, he might not be too happy that it's about to get a whole heck of a lot more personal. And that it's all at the hands of his—" She stopped herself. "You know."

*Wife.* "Yes, I do know."

"I'm right here, honey," Dolly said, touching her back in comfort.

"Just like always." Charlie sent up a prayer of thanks for her friend.

A short time later, she breathed deeply once, twice, and then a third time as she tugged on the drape cord. It opened smoothly. Charlie blinked several times at the popping light bulbs. Even from inside the building, she heard the oohs and ahhs.

Standing off to the side, she watched as several people pointed to the scene before them. A couple, in the trendiest clothes the store offered, dined on what appeared to be the deck of a yacht. The scrumptious fare sat upon the best King's Department Store housewares. The finest linens adorned the beautiful wood dining table.

The dark-haired, broad-shouldered male leaned close to the dark-haired laughing female. Above them read *The Charmings.* But below the title, it had starring *A King and A Royale. A match?*

Fresh, breezy, hip, young and intriguing rang out. A blossoming romance.

The crowd outside seemed to part slightly. Alex shouldered his way through. As he faced the display, he stilled. She couldn't read his expression.

Trepidation filled her. How would he react?

As the photographers quickly grasped the situation, they began taking picture after picture of Alex as he took in every detail. Finally, Alex looked at her in the shadows.

With bated breath and her heart pounding, she walked out of the depths and into the light. Even from where she stood, buffeted by the pane of glass, she caught the gasps of the onlookers.

"Mr. Royale, do you care to comment?"

Another person piped up, "Are you and Ms. King dating, sir?"

Question after question was fired at him. He didn't say a word. He stared at her, long and lingering. A smile tugged at the corner of his mouth.

Her heart stilled.

He bowed his head slightly. She took it as a nod of approval.

"What's going on?" Dolly whispered loudly.

"He's not mad," she threw over her shoulder.

When she looked back, he'd disappeared. The photographers trailed him, still peppering him with questions.

"The second window." Charlie rushed back to the steps. "Come on, he's on the move."

"Huh?" Dolly's question sailed past her as she rushed through the throngs of employees, their claps echoing and bouncing off the marble surrounding them.

"Thank you," Charlie said, pressing her way to the other side of the aisle way and to the second display window.

She met Peg at the landing. "They love it," her assistant gushed.

Charlie rushed on and gained the stairs. She searched the crowd outside the window. She didn't spot Alex. Growing concerned, she stepped closer. More people seemed to have gathered and were now openly chuckling at the smartly dressed couple on King's best quality, hand-crafted furniture. The male fanned out the bogus deck of cards. The female plucked the middle one. All aces. All hearts.

She strained to see over the snapping photographers and to the edge of the crowd. He was nowhere in sight.

"If you're looking for me, I'm right here." His softly spoken words came from just behind her.

Slowly, she turned. She heard the gasps from the growing cluster of people. It seemed as if they then held their collective breaths.

"Alex." His name came out in a hurry. The rush of blood pounded in her ears.

He drew closer. "Is that all you're going to say?"

His expression remained neutral. Beyond him, she heard her staff's whispers of speculation.

"Do you like it?" she asked, too anxious to wait another moment.

He laughed, breaking the trance of the spellbound crowd gathered outside. The flashes went off as he cupped her face in his hands. "Brilliant," he murmured, "absolutely brilliant."

Relief washed over her. Giddiness seemed to follow. "Are you talking about you or me?"

"Both of us, my love, both of us."

# CHAPTER 15

"Dexter's coming," Dolly hissed as Charlie, followed by Alex, descended the display window stairs.

Panic gnawed at her middle. "Dex?!" Her voice rose an octave.

Her staff applauded again, yet somehow the celebration seemed a little less happy with the prospect of what she would soon encounter.

Suddenly, the crowd seemed to grow quiet as they slowly parted.

With all the nerve she could muster, Charlie began to walk. Nearly ten more feet and she halted at the sight.

Fair-haired and with thick, dark-framed glasses, Dexter glared at her. His set jaw and clenched lips spoke volumes. Even in his white, lab coat he couldn't mask the disheveled air about him. The shaggy hair, the slight stubble, and wrinkled jacket all bore the fact that Dexter Snodgrass never gave a hoot about appearances.

Charlie cringed. That could definitely be a problem. She sensed he'd block out their audience and would launch into a heated discussion right then and there.

The strong presence at her back and steadying hand on her arm had Charlie releasing her pent-up breath.

\*\*\*

Alex took in the man standing before his wife. A twinge of compassion hit him. It could easily have been him in that position, jilted. "Dexter, I take it?"

The man nearly gaped at him. "You!" He turned back to Charlie. "It's true, then? How could you?"

Within seconds, Alex realized this would become a spectacle and, most likely, make the papers. Highly aware of the photographers racing into the building and flashbulbs going off all around him, he steered Charlie away. Next, he said, "Snodgrass, follow us."

Thankfully, the other man didn't question him and soon was close on his heels. At the bank of executive elevators, one of the doors opened instantly. "Thank you," Alex muttered to no one in particular.

Once Charlie, Dexter, and he were in the confining space, Alex pressed the button to close the door, blocking them from the curious onlookers.

Silence reined. Tension grew.

Alex looked from the seething man to his chagrined wife. Neither spoke. Neither seemed capable of beginning.

"Charlie," he prompted softly.

Turning to him, she looked like a deer caught in headlights.

"You can do this."

She blew out a heavy breath. Looking back at the scientist, she said, "Dexter, I'm sorry—"

"Sorry? Sorry?! Is that all you can say?" He thumped a fist against his chest. "I worked night and day on anything you needed. Lately, all I've done is sleep, eat, and dream about your stupid perfume. I thought we had something. A connection. What a fool I've been. You never gave a damn about me, did you? All you wanted was to save this godforsaken business at any cost. You used me."

Alex winced at the anger directed at Charlie. She stood there, taking it. God, he admired her so much.

"You're wrong," she replied quietly once he'd stopped to draw in a breath. She swiped away a fast falling tear. "I never meant to hurt you."

That had Dexter jerking back. He sighed wearily, whipping off his glasses and rubbing his eyes. The truth must have sunk in. "How could you? I poured everything into this place. I got so caught up in your enthusiasm for your dream of bringing back this store."

"I never promised you more—"

"Then friends?" he snared. "Just friends."

"You wanted something I couldn't give you. And yes, you are my friend."

He snorted.

With the door still firmly shut, Alex crossed his arms over his chest. "Hey, buddy, give her a chance."

The man glanced over at him. "Funny, I don't think you'd be as charitable if you were in my place."

Alex nodded in understanding. "Point taken."

"You're a lot nicer than I thought you'd be."

Charlie chuckled. "Me, too."

"Hey," Alex said, frowning at her.

She looked at him with her eyebrows raised. "Nice. Sincere. You know, not cheesy."

He grinned. "Or fake." He recalled the words she'd flung at him only a few short weeks ago.

She giggled. Heat stole over him. Her eyes darkened and her cheeks flushed. The ache inside him grew.

Someone cleared their throat. "Ah, excuse me, but I'm still here." Dexter's voice pulled Alex out of his thoughts.

Guilt stained Charlie's skin now. She bit her lip. Alex longed to kiss it and make it better.

"It's true." Resignation echoed in Dexter's voice.

"Yes," Alex answered. "We're—"

Charlie turned sharply to glare at him.

"Friends. Close friends," he amended, highly aware she wanted to keep their marriage a secret for a little bit longer.

"Engaged, secretly, weeks ago," she corrected, briefly waving the diamond-circled ring she wore on her right hand.

"Damn," the mad scientist muttered. The color drained from his face. "And double damn."

Alex sympathized. "I'd be saying a lot worse if I were in your shoes."

"What is it about you and the shoes?" Charlie asked with a smile in her voice.

Alex chuckled, and then shrugged. "What can I say?"

Looking at him, she raised an eyebrow. "Shoe fetish, perhaps?"

"Hey, hey, hey," Dexter interrupted. "No fetishes, please. Don't worry, I get it, all right? You and him." He shivered noticeably. "This is getting too much for me. Let me outta here."

"Gladly." Alex moved to open the door.

Charlie's hand covered his. "Wait." She turned to the other man. "You'll still work for King's, still finish the perfume, still be the creative genius you've always been?"

He sighed heavily. "I'll finish the perfume. I can't promise anything else right now." The hurt echoed in his voice.

"Understood," Charlie said softly. "I'm sorry, Dex."

"Me too, Charlie, me too."

Once Dexter exited, Alex waved for Charlie to precede him. She drew near and then reached over and pressed the close door button.

He sucked in a sharp breath. They were alone. "Did you forget something?" His voice came out low and husky.

Stepping into his arms, she quivered. "A hug?" He pulled her close. When she sank into him, his heart picked up tempo.

"Are there cameras in here?" he asked as he nibbled her earlobe.

"Unfortunately," she murmured. "Just a kiss. A soft, lingering, deep kiss? A kiss won't hurt, will it?"

\*\*\*

Alex took one last admiring look at the window displays. "The Charmings. What will she think of next?" he asked as he settled in the back seat of his car.

Edward scratched his head. "Your guess is as good as mine, sir."

"We'll just have to wait and see, my friend."

"Or I could try to loosen up Dolly's tongue and have her spill it to me." Edward seemed to like the idea too much.

Alex chuckled. "I can't seem to erase that visual, so I'd rather not have any more. I'll just wait and see. I never knew I liked surprises so much."

"Never did before."

"Strange, isn't it? How much a person doesn't even know themselves," he wondered aloud.

"Women!" Edward muttered and then laughed.

\*\*\*

Once away from the comfort of the car, darkness surrounded Charlotte as she, with Edward at her side, made her way to the lone spotlight at the back door of Alex's house. Warm, buttery light poured out of the kitchen windows, like a welcome sign. Her heart hitched at the sight. "Thanks, Edward, for picking me up tonight and having a car waiting for me every night this last week."

"No problem, Miss, or should I say Mrs.?"

She glanced over at him. In the shadows, she made out  the grin that flashed across his face. "Charlie will do just fine."

"Sure thing. Mr. Alex wanted to make sure you got home safe and sound."

A spark of tenderness warmed her middle. "That's so sweet," she said more to herself than to him.

"I'll tell him you said so, ma'am," the driver said with a smile in his voice.

"Never been called that before, has he?"

"Nope, not a once that I can recall."

Her interest piqued. "How long have you known him, Edward?"

"Years." The word was short and to the point, but she sensed the kinship behind it.

"Close, huh?"

"Just like you and Dolly, ma'am."

She sighed. "That's nice to know. I'm glad he had someone all these years."

Now at the door, he got out his key.

"Coming in?"

He pulled back slightly, as if surprised.

"Join us. Dolly always has something delicious waiting for me. I could use a dinner mate."

The grin was back, wider than before. She was certain it had more to do with Dolly than anything else.

As he opened the door and let her precede him, she asked, "Edward, what exactly are your intentions with Dolly anyway?"

He must have heard the laughter in her voice; he chuckled. "Ma'am?"

She swatted his arm. "Don't pretend you didn't hear me."

Just then, Charlie sensed, rather than heard, movement in the kitchen. Going into the big, modern room with all the latest stainless-steel appliances, she stopped short at the sight before her.

Edward nearly ran into her.

Standing at the stove, in jeans and with his sleeves rolled up, Alex stirred whatever was in the medium-sized pot.

"That's it, Mr. R., don't let that burn," Dolly directed as she rinsed off a spoon at the sink.

Charlie suppressed a giggle. Behind her, Edward began to chuckle. In unison, Alex and Dolly turned to the noise.

Alex shrugged self-consciously.

Moving into the room, Charlie went to Dolly, kissing her on the cheek. "You are a miracle worker, my friend," she said quietly.

"Aw shucks."

"Hey," Alex called out, "don't I get one of those, too? Isn't it kiss the cook day or something?"

She giggled. "If it isn't, we'll make it so." Once she was beside him, she stood on tip toe, placing a tender kiss on his cheek. "Yummy, apples and cinnamon."

"That's the ice-cream flavor, not him," Dolly chastised. "Apple pie ice cream, you like?"

"I like," Edward said.

"Hey, you forgetting something?" she teased.

The driver looked perplexed.

"A kiss. You know, for the cook."

He actually blushed, but went over and gave her a light peck on the cheek.

"More later, Eddie?"

"Yes, ma'am." He turned to Alex, looking uncomfortable. "You want one too, sir?"

Charlie laughed and the others joined in.

Hours later, Charlie glanced around at the three people sitting with her at the kitchen table. In one hand, they all held the cards they were dealt, while in the other they held a spoon to dip into the newest ice cream concoction Dolly and Alex had created. It felt like home.

Dolly splayed out another winning hand.

"Card shark," Eddie muttered as he tossed down his cards and went back to the bowl in front of him.

"Always have been," Dolly said, raking in the pot, the metal jingling. The pile of coins in front of her kept growing.

"Always will be," Charlie pointed out.

She caught Alex's glance. He winked. Heat stole over her cheeks.

All evening she'd watched as his smile came often. Easy banter flowed among them. Thankfully, gone were all signs of the stuffy businessman and in its place was a very sexy, very down-to-earth man. Now, this was the husband she never knew she wanted.

In the back of her mind, she wondered if she could hold onto this forever.

*** 

A week later, Alex shuffled the papers on his desk in his study. He checked his watch once again. "After ten," he muttered. "Where could she be?" He didn't need a psychic to answer that one. Work.

He leaned back in his chair and rested his feet on the edge of the desk, ankles crossed. "A work widower."

He closed his eyes and pictured her. Her enthusiasm was contagious. Each morning she'd sit across from him at breakfast and beam. Her eyes sparkled and her smile came even easier than usual. He especially adored her playfulness.

And, when he popped in to see her at her work, he respected her air of confidence and quick decision-making skills. But, most of all, he admired the way she treated the people who worked for her. Correction, worked with her, as Charlie pointed out time and time again.

She was more than he'd ever hoped for, more than he knew he'd needed. Charlie made him want to be a better friend, a better husband, a better man.

Smiling, he allowed himself to recall their time together. His thoughts lingered on their wedding night. So soft, so warm, and so willing. He groaned softly.

"What, may I ask, are you thinking?" Charlie asked.

Alex opened his eyes, wondering if she was real or just part of his very vivid imagination.

Rushing into the room, she dropped her purse and tote bag in a nearby chair. Soon she rounded the desk. "May I?" she asked, lifting his arms and gingerly seating herself in his lap, and then wrapping his arms around her.

"I didn't even get to answer." He gathered her close, welcoming her warmth. He inhaled deep. Her perfume tickled his senses.

"Complaining?" She snuggled into him. Her lips brushed the side of his neck. He shivered.

"Never," he moaned.

She giggled.

The sound vibrated through him and he grasped her closer still.

"You are such a good courter. Is that even a word?"

"Me? I believe you are the one throwing yourself at me. Talk about a good courter. And no, it's not a word. But who cares?"

Suddenly, she kissed his cheek repeatedly with quick, hard pecks.

"A little more to the left, please."

"Your left or mine?"

"Mine."

She halted a few inches away from his lips. As she stared into his eyes, his heart tumbled in his chest.

"Charlie," he whispered.

"Alex," she said in an equally breathy voice.

She lowered her lips to his. Gently, she kissed the corner of his mouth, and then the other side. She feathered the lightest of kisses over his lips. She increased the pressure.

Alex brought a hand up to cradle the back of her head, liking the way the silky strands of her hair caressed his skin. She parted his lips with her tongue. He groaned. He heard, as well as felt, her suck in a sharp breath. He moaned this time. She responded, sending a swift, sharp ache crashing through him.

She teased him, first darting her tongue in his mouth, then, ever so gently, tangling hers around his in a wicked, tantalizing dance of promise and desire.

The kiss went on and on. He never wanted it to end.

She reached out with her hands, soft and seeking, to unbutton his shirt. Then she delved her fingers between the parted fabric and blazed a trail of fire over his flesh. He burned.

Still clinging to her kiss, he ran his free hand over her back, waist, hips, and then her perfectly round bottom, down her long thighs, and then back up again. In the back of his mind, he thanked her for wearing the pencil-thin skirt. It fit her like a second skin.

A shiver racked her. His body tightened and hardened in all the right places. Slowly, she pulled away. Her sweet breath fanned over his mouth. He longed to drag her back for more of the same. Her eyes, now a liquid caramel, tried to focus on him.

"Welcome home, wife." He nearly growled the last. He didn't realize how possessive he could be. Her condition of keeping their marriage a secret fueled his desire for the world to know.

"Husband." He heard the smile in her voice.

She knew. She sensed how difficult it had been for him to keep his distance from her out in public, to dodge reporters' questions, to beg his grandparents from revealing the truth, and to appear as if they didn't even live together.

Gates locked and drapes drawn at all hours, and, nearly a prisoner in his own home when he was there, had been his routine of late. How many times had she snuck out the back in the early-morning hours or hurried in during the late-evening hours to side-step the paparazzi? He'd avoided them at the house, trying to send the message he was unavailable there.

And at his office, he'd come out to face them and fob off their many pictures, distracting them from bothering her by telling them Ms. King would not be making any statements.

"Two weeks down, four to go," he said.

"Is that all you can think of right now?" she asked, leaning into him even more.

He smiled as he gazed at her. "Hardly."

She wiggled. He groaned again. "It seems to me," she brushed her lips against his, "husband of mine, hard is definitely the perfect word right now."

"Oh, so you've noticed."

Wrinkling her nose at him, she said, "I'm quick like that."

"Not too quick, I hope," he said, capturing her lips in a long, drugging kiss.

She reluctantly broke the embrace. Charlie's breathing came swift and shallow. It matched his.

The heat of her body, the fullness of her breasts pressed into his chest, the lush curves under his hands all inflamed him.

"I've got all night, Alex. How about you?"

"No financial statements, no window displays, no notes for staff meetings to attend to?" he asked, referring to her many duties that occupied her time recently.

"All done," she said. "And, I'll have you know sales are up."

That piece of knowledge shouldn't surprise him after the amazing response to her ongoing storyline of the Charmings. He brushed aside the sliver of unease at the thought of having to end this charade in a few weeks. Bottom line, it came down to Royale Enterprises couldn't afford to keep King's Department Store going until it turned a real profit. "You're very good."

"Oh, Alex, you'll see just how good I am in a few minutes."

# CHAPTER 16

Courting, as she called it, came easy to him, Charlie thought the next day as she trailed her fingers over her slightly swollen lips. His kisses stirred her like no other. His touch, warm and lingering, set her ablaze.

Gazing into the large mirror with lights surrounding it, she blinked at her reflection. She glowed. There was no denying that fact. Her eyes sparkled, she couldn't stop the ever present tug of a smile, and her skin appeared radiant, if she did say so herself.

Marriage was very, very good to her.

But, if truth be told, it was the man himself that occupied her thoughts and had her gasping for breath on many occasions. Her initial impression of him as stuffy and all business contradicted the man she'd come to know. He had this way about him.

For the first time in years, she belonged.

He didn't laugh well, not hard at her antics or ideas. In fact, the more she allowed him to see her designs and share her thoughts he seemed to be open and surprisingly interested.

She'd even gone so far as make a suggestion or two about his family business. He'd considered it, and then later had mentioned he'd put them in place.

Leaning her elbows on the dressing table, she pressed her fists against her cheeks. "Amazing, isn't he?" she whispered to herself.

"Gorgeous as the first time, honey," Dolly said, coming up behind her. "Who'd have thunk it that you'd be wearing that wedding dress twice in less than three weeks?" she asked in a hushed tone.

Sitting up straight, she asked, "And for a photo shoot at that?" Charlie shook her head. She wore her hair pulled back again. But now she'd added small diamond earrings and a very delicate matching diamond necklace, all courtesy of King's Department Store.

"Ready, Charlie?" Peg asked with a clipboard cradled in her arm.

"Sure thing."

Rico, flamboyant and colorful as ever, came bustling over. He waved his hands around her frame. "Perfecto."

She chuckled. "You might want to bring some powder or even some deodorant if this thing goes on too long."

He whipped out his makeup brush and container of powder. "Got it." Snatching a roll-on from the table in front of her, he said, "B.O., check."

"B.O.?" Dolly and Peg asked in unison.

He rolled his eyes at them and asked. "Body odor. Where have you two been for the last century?"

Charlie watched as they turned to each other and shrugged helplessly.

A few minutes later, as directed, Charlie took the short stool in the center of the photo shoot. Andre, her photographer friend, checked and rechecked the lighting. His assistants fluffed and re-fluffed her gown.

"Is this a King's dress?" one of them asked. Charlie, sitting perfectly still, thought the question came from the short, blonde-haired young woman stooping behind her.

"An original," Dolly piped up. Out of the corner of her eye, Charlie saw her friend wink.

She smiled. Well, not quite a King's design, but close enough. A King did design it and Dolly did make it.

Just then she heard a commotion off the set and beyond the big, bright lights. Several people talked at once.

"Oh, they're here!" Dolly exclaimed.

"Who?" Charlie couldn't make out anyone in the shadows.

"The girls. I called for their dresses and they came!"

"The girls?"

"It's me, Francine. And here's Priscilla. Will you get this guy off of us?" Her stepsister's distinct voice reached her.

"Francie?"

"You know her, them, Charlie?" Rico asked, disgust dripping from his voice.

"We're related," Priscilla chimed in.

He tsked. "Charlie, tell me it's not true."

"It is," she said hesitantly, afraid of his outspokenness.

"No way!"

"Way," Charlie and the girls said in unison.

"Are they in the shoot, too?"

The girls came to the edge of the pristine white floor draping. Charlie blinked several times. What had happened to their new looks? The black clothing was back, even with the thick stockings and clunky shoes. Both of them clutched equally matronly black purses. They had their hair scraped back, held by a thick black headband. And not an ounce of makeup adorned their pretty faces. Charlie groaned inwardly.

"Can we be?" Priscilla asked.

"Not without a whole lotta work," Rico pointed out, plucking at the drab sleeve with two fingers.

"Who else can wear their custom-made dresses, honey?" Dolly asked loudly.

"It's true." Charlie gave in. "Rico, can you give them the works?"

His long-suffering sigh echoed all around her.

"You are the miracle worker, remember?" She bit her lip.

"Of course I am," he declared. "Come on, girls, we have a whole new world to conquer. And I'm the only one man enough who can do it."

An hour later, Charlie's muscles strained with the effort of holding herself in one awkward position after another for long lengths of time.

"Charlie, please," Andre begged. "Smile. Not the wooden one, either."

This required more than she'd anticipated. In her mind, she saw her work piling up on her desk. She had papers to sign, new displays to design, and another staff meeting to conduct on the upcoming sale.

She forced another smile.

He cursed in a foreign language, French she was certain.

"Sorry, I guess I'm just not cut out for this line of work."

"What line? Wife?" Alex asked from the shadows.

Sitting up straight, she sucked in a sharp breath. "Alex?"

Gasps rent the air. Next, she detected the high trill of voices. He seemed to affect most women that way, even Rico. She giggled at that thought.

"That's it," Andre shouted. The sudden rush of cameras clicking pierced the room.

Out of the corner of her eye, she saw her husband walk to the edge of the draping and kick off his shoes. Just the sight of his big, broad-shouldered frame stole her senses away. She shifted slightly to see him more as he slowly walked toward her.

A smile tugged at his lips. "You didn't answer my question," Alex gently reminded her, his eyes twinkling.

"Wife, huh?" She couldn't contain the dreamy quality in her voice. "Oh, I don't know. You'll have to be the judge of that."

More female gasps sliced through the air of giddy anticipation.

He raised an eyebrow. Halting before her, he dropped to one knee. He reached out and trailed a finger over her cheek. "Really? And just how am I supposed to do that?"

"Will you marry me, Alex?"

He laughed. She joined him. His presence, his willingness to tease her and play along with her warmed her to her very soul, leaving an indelible mark on her heart.

She loved him. She finally admitted it to herself. Deeply, irrevocably, she loved her husband.

"Yes, Charlotte King, it would be my pleasure to marry you," he said, and then softly he added, "All over again."

\*\*\*

Sitting in the back of his car, Alex smiled as he fingered the crisp, beautifully crafted cardstock with the delicate swirls of lettering gracing it. She'd done it again. This time, as a form of advertising, Charlie had sent out wedding invitations for the Charmings, the couple she'd invented for her store displays.

She'd played her and Alex's real budding relationship, engagement, and now wedding with perfect precision while tempting the public's interest not only in them, but in King's merchandise as well.

"Good, huh?" Edward asked, glancing in the rearview mirror.

"Amazing," Alex said, still in awe over the way her mind worked. If she'd been at the helm of King's Department Store all these years, it wouldn't be in dire straits now. But, in just a few more weeks, he'd have to pull the plug on the whole thing. A twinge of guilt poked him in his middle.

"We're here, sir." Edward easily maneuvered the town car in front of the store as the uniformed man directed them into the slot. "Looks like the crowd is gathering in anticipation."

Absently, Alex gazed out the window and noted the many people, especially women, milling about. The first window had been revealed. He strained to see the display. No such luck. The "ceremony" started at ten a.m. He checked his watch. Fifteen minutes to go. He could sneak in and see Charlie first. Would he ruin it for her, though?

"I could go around the block another turn."

"No, no." He dismissed his friend's offer. "I don't want to miss it." He reconsidered his position and decided to throw caution to the wind and get out of the car. After all, he had to check out the first window. He wondered what she'd dreamed up for that one.

He grabbed for the door handle. The car phone rang.

"Shall I get that?"

"No, Edward, let it ring."

"It's your grandfather," Edward said, lifting up the phone to show Alex the caller ID.

He blew out a hot breath. The phone rang over and over again. Giving in, he snatched up his extension. With forced cheer, he said, "Grandfather, how are you?"

"Where in the devil have you been, son?"

He knew the older man just wasn't asking about the present moment. "I've been—"

"Distracted? I realize you just got married, but, son, you spend more time at her store than you do in your own office."

"That's not entirely true, sir." He grimaced at his own defensiveness.

"Stop, Albert, your heart." Alex heard his grandmother in the background. "Alex," her voice grew louder, "tell your grandfather he's got nothing to worry about. You'll take care of everything just like you always do."

"Honey, I've got this." Gramps obviously spoke to his wife.

"Oh, Albert, tell him about the party." Her voice faded out, and then came on the line. "Alex, are you there? We're going to throw you and Charlotte a reception. Saturday, sweetheart. That's the perfect way to end this silly charade with the press."

"Gran—"

"No need to thank us. You know how I just love parties. Oh, won't it be wonderful, the first time as a family we officially introduce your wife, Charlotte Royale?"

What would Charlie say about the fuss? "She's still a King."

"I suppose I have to invite the stepmother." He pictured her gnawing on a painted fingernail. "It wouldn't be polite if I didn't."

"And the sisters," he pointed out absently, suppressing a chuckle at the absurdity of the conversation. He realized he hated parties. On any given night or day, he'd rather be alone with Charlie.

"Oh yes. I can't imagine they'd bring dates, do you? I'll just make sure there's a few extra seats just in case." She seemed lost in thought now.

Suddenly, his grandfather's voice rumbled in his ear as if they'd never been interrupted. "I see the newspapers, my boy. I've seen the pictures of you and her at King's. What in the blue blazes has she done to you?"

His grandmother cried out in the background, "The window displays! Tell Charlotte the Charmings are wonderful!"

A smile tugged at the corner of his mouth. Just wait until they saw him in the wedding ads. For the first time ever, he hadn't minded a photographer taking his picture, especially with his wife. He'd willingly signed the consent form to help Charlie.

He wanted her to succeed. If only for a short time until he had to sell the store.

"And I know just how much time you spend away from Royale Enterprises." His grandfather's words had him jerking back to reality. "Don't you think I know what's going on in the business I started?" Hurt and disappointment shadowed his words.

Something kicked Alex in his chest. He never wanted to let his grandfather down. "Chadwick."

"At least you still remember his name."

"Grandfather, he's been gunning to take over since before you semi-retired." For years, Alex had been five steps ahead of Chadwick. Now, it seemed, he'd let his guard down and the shark had moved in.

"Yes, he's got a one-track mind. And that's what we need now more than ever."

"So what has he been telling you?"

"You sent Stuart to California when you should have gone yourself. We lost the deal."

Sitting up straighter, Alex reached for his briefcase. He snapped it open and yanked out a file. "Why wasn't

I notified?" He flipped through the pages. "Stuart's report mentioned nothing of any discontent. He says he had them eating out of his hand."

He'd checked and rechecked the progress report and the notes. He'd grilled Stuart himself.

"You didn't go yourself. They felt if the top dog at Royale Enterprises wasn't interested enough in them, why should they give us their business? You know we have to baby these people. You offended the very company that would have brought in millions over the next two years. And, to top it all off, you nearly bankrupt Royale Enterprises to buy King's Department Store."

His heart sank. His grandfather had found out. "I can explain."

"Hah! Have you lost your mind, son?"

"Please, Albert, don't upset yourself so," he heard his grandmother call out. "Trust Alex; he'll make it all right, won't you, dear?"

His grandfather continued, "We're in the business of developing upscale shopping malls in the wealthiest communities, not set up shop to sell wares."

Alex squeezed his eyes shut. He felt the muscle in his jaw jump to life. "It's only temporary. I intend to sell it. All the media attention is causing business to pick up. That means I buy low and sell high, Grandfather."

Some of the bluster seemed to go out of the older man. "Why didn't you say something?"

"I didn't want you to be this upset."

He snorted. "Too late." His long, heavy sigh caused another pang of guilt to shoot through Alex.

"I'm sorry. Some day I'll tell you everything. But, for now, let me do it my way."

"When?"

"When?"

"Yes, son, when are you going to put that beast up for sale?"

"Soon. A couple of weeks," he admitted, recalling his assistant's discreet, tentative inquiries into selling King's. They already had a few interested companies, more with each successful sales campaign. Thoughts of Charlie rushed through his mind. Something strong and heavy clamped down in his chest.

"Make it quick." For a long moment there was silence. "Alex, you've got a business to run, not a store to babysit. You decide if you want to continue at Royale Enterprises or play shopkeeper." Sadness crept into his voice. "I'm an old man who doesn't have much time left. Give your grandmother and me a great-grandchild. And don't disappoint me in losing all I've built these years. That includes my hopes and dreams of you and your son continuing on where I left off. It's either King's or Royale Enterprises. You can't have both."

# CHAPTER 17

The finality of his grandfather's words rang in his ears as Alex hung up. But it was the deep well of disappointment in Gramps' voice that broke his heart. "You can't have both," Alex repeated, gritting his teeth.

"That bad?"

"Worse, my friend, much worse." Alex blew out a hot breath. He had a decision to make. It wasn't going to be pretty.

After frantic phone calls to his assistant and Stuart, Alex finally exited the car nearly twenty minutes later. He made his way into the store as the familiar doorman spotted Alex and had ushered him through the growing crowd after Alex had viewed both window displays.

He smiled wistfully as he recalled the first one with Charlie, in a dressing gown, getting ready at the vanity table while her stepsisters exchanged shoes and Dolly sat in a nearby chair completing the last stitches on a hem.

The second one... Breathtaking, he thought. Flowers adorned the makeshift garden. White gauzy fabric draped the wedding altar. Stunning, Charlie stood in her wedding dress. Beside her, he cupped her face in his palms, ready to kiss her.

Still lost in thought, he entered King's. He stopped in his tracks. Gone were the classic racks upon racks of clothes, the soft strains of elevator music, and stiff mannequins dressed in all-too-boring business attire. Even the lighting had been adjusted. Everything seemed brighter and warmer. As another popular love song came on, he heard several women nearby exclaim at the rich, husky voice of the well-known singer.

He glanced around in fascinated wonder at the transformation. The white-draped fabric and flowers continued throughout the store. Seating arrangements had been created, as if this were a real wedding reception. A five-tier wedding cake with King's gift bags on the table took up one area.

His jaw nearly dropped as saleswomen, posing as wait staff, served wedding cake in neat little lavender take-home boxes with King's Department Store crown logo imprinted on the top, along with sparkling liquid in champagne glasses. Behind the servers were models, posing in their colorful hip outfits, while salespeople with an armful of clothes whisked away women to the dressing areas.

"What do you think?" Charlie asked as she suddenly appeared by his side.

She seemed to glow. "You, my love, are amazing."

"I know that. I meant the store."

He chuckled. "Chic. Unique. Yet intimate. I would say you are a genius."

Her cheeks turned pink. She waved a hand to indicate the employees working behind her. "My team is." On tiptoe, she leaned close and kissed him on the cheek. "Thank you, Alex."

"For what?" He honestly had no clue what she was talking about.

"For giving me time."

Alex swallowed hard.

"Time away from you, so I could be here to help with all this planning and work," she said, and then slipped her arm through his. "I think we're drawing too much attention," she whispered as he became aware of the many stares.

Women of all ages, shapes, and sizes seemed to stop their shopping to focus on them. Most smiled, others giggled, while some even raised their glasses in a toast.

"Ladies," he said, nodding their way.

"Shall I show you the rest?"

He looked at her, raising an eyebrow. "Rest of what?"

"You'll see." Promise echoed in her words.

Groaning, he followed her lead.

This time she giggled. "Not that," she said in mock horror.

A moment later, he realized where they were going. Getting closer, there was no way to ignore the huge posters hanging behind the jewelry counter and the nearby salon.

He gulped. "Charlie."

There, in more than eight-foot glory, his wife's picture hung. The close-up of her looking off to her right as she smiled warmly captured her bare shoulders just above the neckline of her wedding dress, spotlighting the diamond earrings and necklace.

In the back of his mind, he noted the other photos in the surrounding area. He glanced at the close-up photo where he slipped her wedding ring onto her left ring finger, there to stay. However, he couldn't seem to yank his gaze away from the full shot of both of them; he was in profile as he kneeled before her and she gazed lovingly at him.

"Pretty good, if I do say so myself."

A bolt of electricity zapped through his body. He saw it for the very first time. She loved him. And he loved her. The picture couldn't lie. "Perfect," he said absently. "Simply, utterly perfect."

He knew he'd treasure this moment for the rest of his life.

"Sir, I'm sorry to interrupt," Edward's voice intruded from beside him, "but you have a plane to catch."

Whatever he'd dreamed about for a future for Charlie and himself seemed to crash right before him.

"Alex, a plane?" He heard the hurt in her tone.

Grimly, he turned to her. There, in her eyes, bore the well of disappointment. His middle clenched. "I've got to go to California."

"Now?"

He blew out a hot breath. "I'm afraid so. Business." He had to save the deal and Royale Enterprises all in one shot. After all, wasn't his grandparents and what they longed for his first priority? It always had been. And it always would be for him. "Walk me to the car?" he asked softly, dreading the inevitable.

\*\*\*

Outside, standing beside the car door, Charlie noted the strain in his eyes. "Is everything all right?"

Instead of answering, he gathered her close. She melted into him, savoring the warmth and strength of his arms surrounding her and his big solid chest protecting her. She sighed. He held her tighter.

"I'm sorry, Charlie," he whispered in her ear, "for doing this to you."

A sense of unease made her shiver. Why did it sound like he was apologizing for more than just this sudden trip? She pulled away slightly to look up into his eyes again. They were clouded. He seemed troubled. "Alex, please tell me what's really going on."

A sad smile tugged at his mouth. With what appeared to be forced cheer, he said, "A party. Well, a reception. My grandparents insist on introducing us properly to the world, I'm afraid. Saturday night. I'll be back just in time. I'll have my assistant call you with all the details."

"A party?"

"I know, I hate them, too." He kissed her quick, and then made to let go.

"Wait, not so fast." She hated the desperate quality in her voice. He came back fully to her. "Kiss me, please. A real one."

"My pleasure, beautiful."

Slowly, he dipped his head. Charlie closed her eyes and welcomed the warm, firm pressure of his mouth against hers. She didn't want it to end. The shelter of his embrace gave her a false sense of security and reassurance.

In the background, she became aware of the claps, cheers, and even some cameras clicking away. They had an audience. Again.

Reluctantly, she broke the kiss, sighing heavily. With one last look, he got into the back seat. He grabbed a nearby file and flipped through the pages, becoming instantly absorbed in the material. He didn't even glance at her as Edward drove away.

Her heart sank. She'd just gotten a glimpse of the old Alex. Stiff, business-like, and shut down. She had five days to figure out why this sudden change in him and the urgent need to fly off to conduct business he'd never mentioned previously. But would she like the answer?

\*\*\*

Charlie leaned her forehead against the cool window pane as she sat in her office window seat. Friday night after nine and the stillness surrounding her should be welcome. But it wasn't.

She tugged the fuzzy throw a little bit more over her shoulder. The soft rustle of her sketch pad shifting reminded her she still had to finish the details on the perfume box for King's new scent, Charming.

The echoing silence in the executive offices indoors combated with the sound of rain dripping down the windows outside.

"Sad. Lonely," she whispered as her middle knotted again. She couldn't call her friend. Dolly had a date with Edward. "All alone." Tears smarted her eyes.

It had been four long nights without Alex. Brief, distracted calls made it even more unbearable. Her husband had suddenly become a stranger to her.

And, to be honest, Charlie didn't particularly like the change.

Funny how a few short weeks ago she'd never thought of anything but the store. Now, thoughts of Alex were always in the back of her mind, especially now that he was so remote.

Sighing heavily, she berated herself. She'd gone and fallen in love with him. An ache shot through her. "Yes, I love my husband," she said softly, trying out the words aloud for the first time. "Fully, deeply, painfully in love." But she didn't have to like the business man who'd snuck back in and stole him away.

Her tummy twisted again. She couldn't recall the last time she'd stopped to take a bite. Wrinkling her nose at the thought of food, she realized she didn't have the stomach for it. Charlie giggled at her own pun.

"You are so sorry, girl."

She must have dozed off, because the next thing she was aware of was sounds in the outer office. Sitting up, she recognized Bruno's, the night guard, voice. Then another male answered.

"Alex?" she called out, her heart hitching. She brushed aside her sketch pad and threw off the blanket.

Suddenly, his presence filled the doorframe. He moved closer. "Should I call you Sleeping Beauty now?"

Smiling, she rubbed at her eyes. "Something like that."

"Miss Charlie, I found this man lurking around the building." Bruno nodded to her husband and the bag he was carrying as the guard came into the room. "I only let him in 'cause he brought dinner." He winked at her. "Miss Dolly's famous chicken soup."

Her stomach growled. She pressed a hand to her middle. "Yummy. Have some with us."

"You know she fixed me up, too." He smacked his lips. "And dumplings."

"Oh, my gosh. I'm famished."

"If you weren't before, you should be now," Bruno said. "Dolly's one mean cook. You know if I wasn't married, I would have snatched her up long ago."

Charlie smiled. "Hah! It's not just her cooking. It's because of her winning streak at poker. You, my friend, would've been one rich man."

He laughed heartily, shaking his head. "Dang that woman! She could beat the pants off any man she played with. Your daddy, the guys, and me would be crying by the end of the night."

She smiled warmly at the many stories of their late night poker games in the guard room downstairs.

"All right to leave this man with you, miss?" She detected the hint of protectiveness.

"Did you pat him down? Maybe he's packing heat," she teased.

"Oh, I was gonna leave that up to you, Miss Charlie."

She laughed. "I can handle that."

A slight awkwardness descended as Bruno strolled away, whistling.

For the first time, she looked directly at her husband. A questioning look shadowed his features.

"Alex."

"Charlie."

Tucking the blanket around her, she settled in again. She moved her papers and sketch pad from the seat and plopped them on the floor beside her. "Would you like to join me?"

The formality didn't seem lost on him. "Thank you."

He made his way around her desk and came closer. She stole glimpses of him. Tall and breathtaking as always, she mused. Her heart skipped a beat as the scent of him tickled her senses. Still in his business attire, she wondered if he'd come straight from a meeting.

"Oh, I think we have Dolly to thank for this." When he sat beside her, she helped him pull out the food containers. She snatched up a spoon. Taking the lid off, she dipped into the steaming liquid, and then tasted a bite. She moaned. "Delish!"

He joined her, echoing her sentiments.

"But I thought she had a date."

Shrugging, he said, "Change of plans. The rain. Me coming home a day early."

Curiosity won out. "Why?"

"Why not? I wrapped up the first phase of business late today."

"First phase?" She didn't like the sound of this.

"I go back Monday." She noted the tiredness in his tone.

Disappointed, she said, "Oh, that's right, the party."

He murmured his agreement. She felt an icy stab of pain somewhere in her chest.

"Do you mind?"

Lost in thought, she jerked her head up. "Huh?"

Tugging at his tie, he asked, "This?"

She swallowed hard, thinking he didn't have to stop with just that piece of clothing. He handed her his container of soup.

Gingerly, she took it from him. He shucked off his suit jacket. "And this?"

An ache, deep and low, shot through her. She broke the stare.

Gazing out at the rain slicked window, she focused on the yellowy lights coming from the streetlight below. She heard metal clink together and realized he'd just removed his cuff links. The whisper of fabric clued her into his rolling up his sleeves.

For a brief moment, she closed her eyes and remembered his naked chest beneath her fingers. She groaned inwardly.

"Better."

Coming back to the moment, she glanced his way as she smiled tightly. *Wrong move.* His hot, dark stare burned into her. The searing imprint shook her to her core. She wanted him. Wanted what they'd had, even if only for a few stolen minutes.

His hand brushed against hers as he relieved her of the container. Once free of the soup, she curled her fingers into her palm, hoping to capture the feel of his skin. She shook her head at what she longed for but may never have again. Where had her Alex gone?

Having lost her appetite, she offered him her soup.

"Not hungry? Dolly said you haven't been eating lately."

Why would her friend tell him that? Not on purpose, she reasoned. This time, she shrugged, as she tugged at the fringe on the blanket. "Business. Too busy. Too distracted." She didn't dare tell him the complete truth. Because she missed him terribly.

"Dexter?"

He almost sounded jealous. She shook it off. "Thankfully, he's been working around the clock to finish the perfume. I'm grateful for all his help. You know, he's a genius—"

"So I've heard."

"When it comes to formulas and potions," she added, frowning at the dark look chasing across his features. "I wish he'd stay. I think he really cares about this place succeeding almost as much as I do."

"Tell me something I don't know."

Charlie refused to be drawn into a debate over Dexter's merits. Instead, she gave into Alex's wishes. "Well, I don't think you know I was born here."

"Dallas? But I thought…" He seemed puzzled.

"No, here. In this office." She waited for his response.

He didn't make her wait long. "Here here?"

At his utter look of astonishment, she chuckled. She pointed at him. "You should see the look on your face."

He joined her in laughter.

The tension eased. She breathed a sigh of relief. Visions of the Alex she'd come to know and love peeked out behind the business mask.

"Don't keep me hanging, tell me," he pleaded.

"If you insist." She seemed to tumble back in time as she glanced around the office space. "This was my father's office. It looked different then. Well, not the desk, that's the same. I saved it," she said wistfully, biting her lip. She tossed off a wave of melancholy, and then continued. "Dusty, cluttered, you name it, Dolly described it."

"She's been with your family that long?"

"We met the day I was born." She heard the warmth in her own voice. "Let me start at the beginning. My dad was working, as usual, and my mom was big and round with me. She had her arms loaded with shopping bags when the first contraction came. No one would stop to help her as she made her way here, trying to get to my dad. Don't you know, while Dolly waited to catch the bus back to her boss, she saw my mom. Dolly knew if she didn't get back in time to serve lunch she'd be fired, but she couldn't just leave my mom."

"She stopped to help," he said, nodding in understanding.

Charlie giggled, knowing she was talking way too fast, but continued. "As the story goes, my mother, and her packages, weighed a ton. Dolly tried to keep the dry cleaning bag from dragging and the clothes in it from getting wrinkled. In her other arm, she clutched the sack of vegetables as she tried to half carry my mother here while my mom hung on for dear life to her own shopping bags. Baby things, can you believe it?"

He smiled widely and shook his head.

"Dolly soon gave up on the dry cleaning and the veggies."

"But not your mom."

"Nope, thankfully. Long story short, from the moment she hit King's door, she shouted, 'Mr. K., Mr. K., I got your wife and she's about to have your baby.' Well, word spread like lightning and Daddy came rushing downstairs. Then he and Dolly had a heated debate over whether or not my mother could make it to the hospital in time."

"Let me guess. Dolly won."

"Bingo." She clapped her hands. "To top it off, Dolly pointed out if he didn't want the whole store to see, they better get my mom some privacy and pronto." She waved a hand over the room. "And presto, less than fifteen minutes later I was born on the floor just over there."

He stared at the spot she indicated, blinking several times. "Right there?"

"Yep. So when I say King's is home to me, I truly mean it."

She swore he paled.

"Alex, you okay?"

Glancing down at the food container, he said quietly, "I think I just lost my appetite, too."

Somehow she didn't think it had anything to do with a queasy stomach at the vision of her birth. A shiver of disquiet slithered down her spine. Why would he get upset after she said she truly meant King's was her home? Unless…

# CHAPTER 18

Alex paced the ballroom. People stared. He didn't really care.

Several women had already come up to converse. A few even touched his arm briefly. The bold ones tried to slip him their card. He'd strongly, yet politely, declined.

"Where is she?" he wondered aloud.

"Son, what did you do, go and lose your bride already?" His grandfather patted him on the shoulder.

Smiling weakly, he said, "It appears that way."

His grandmother, in a shimmering blue gown and her white hair perfectly styled, joined them. "Don't be silly, she's just a little late. Why, Alex, didn't you tell me she was working late?"

"Yes, a new ad campaign," he answered, distracted. "Some makeovers or something next week."

"Makeovers? Really?" His grandmother's interest piqued.

He glanced at his watch. Quarter to nine. "Where could she be?"

The starch in his collar seemed to strangle him. The longer he waited, the more it tightened around his neck, along with the bow tie to his tux. He hated parties. He thought he'd put an end to the stiff, boring awkward chitchat of these get-togethers once he married. Apparently, he was wrong.

Gasps rent the air. Alex turned quickly. Through the crowd, he spotted her immediately. She took his breath away. A well of love crashed down on him, shaking him. He'd never thought he could feel this way about a woman.

The marriage should have been conducted in a business-like manner. Cool, calm, and beneficial to both of them. An arrangement. That had been his intention all along.

He failed miserably.

The guests near the doorway parted politely as Charlie walked into the room. The men couldn't keep their eyes off of her. He sensed some of the women eyeing her coldly. Jealous, he thought.

She glanced around and then halted when she spotted him. To the others, she must have seemed at ease for all the grace she possessed. But, he noted the wooden smile and the slight tremor in her cheek.

A well of empathy rose in him. Alex shouldered his way to Charlie. Getting closer, he heard the surprise in people's voices. Once the older couple in front of him stood back, he had little wonder as to what the shock was all about.

In the back of his mind, he heard the whirl of cameras.

There, walking toward him, Charlie, with her hair pulled back, wore the most revealing dress he'd ever seen at one of these formal affairs.

He gulped hard.

The rich maroon, velvety two-piece outfit fit her like a second skin. The top came to her neck, almost like a turtleneck and had long sleeves. But it ended just below her breasts, making them stand out even more. From the bottom, dangling beads grazed her bare middle. He groaned as he dropped his eyes to her silky flesh, past her delicate navel and skimmed over her hips. The skirt began there, low and snug, with matching beads attached, and there was a deep slit up the side, baring her long, gorgeous legs.

Heat coiled in his middle. "Sweet Jesus," he muttered.

"Amen," a male voice said off to his right.

Getting near, he reached out to her. She placed her hand in his as he captured her stare. He caught the smile lingering there and something more. Heat rose. "Charlie."

"Alex." He detected the hint of relief.

He tugged gently and she came all the way into his arms.

He brushed his fingers along her waist. He felt her shiver in his arms. His body ached. Tentatively, she closed her eyes. Alex gathered her closer still. At the touch of her hands circling his shoulders, desire licked at his blood. He gave in to the demanding need to kiss her. Her lips parted on a small gasp. He groaned, and then deepened the kiss.

If anyone asked, he would have no idea just how long he held her. He lost all track of time and place. It had been far too long since he'd done this. He never wanted it to end. If he wasn't mistaken, she didn't either.

"Alex, Alex!" Slowly he became aware of his grandmother's cries.

Reluctantly, he ended the embrace, taking his time to pull back from his wife. Her eyes, dark and luminous, haunted him. She wanted him as much as he wanted her. There was no doubt about it.

"Please, Alex," his grandmother pleaded, her voice full of embarrassment.

Some woman said, "I knew it was real."

"No, you didn't," another woman's voice chastised her. "Everyone, including you, thought it was a set-up."

A gruff male voice joined in, "Well, now we know differently, don't we?"

"There's no faking that," a younger woman said with a hint of envy.

Suddenly, Alex came back to reality with a hard thud. Never in his life had he lost complete and utter control of his senses. He'd been schooled from a youngster to behave, especially in public, and most especially in front of the press.

He wanted nothing more than to lift his wife in his arms and carry her off to bed. Damn this shindig and damn appearances, he cursed silently.

Gazing at her now, warmth spread. But there was a fusion of shock that rushed through him, also. He hadn't bargained on this. He hadn't anticipated the deep, constant ache for her. Not just making love to her, but being with her.

He'd had a safe, boring life before Charlie. His heart had been intact, and, he thought, would remain so even after marriage. It was just a simple arrangement. They'd marry and have at least one child. Oh, and he had to court her. What was so difficult about that?

But she'd turned his world upside down.

As his grandfather had asked him on the phone this week, what in the blue blazes had Charlie done to him?

\*\*\*

Charlie wondered how she'd made it this long through the reception. His grandparents were lovely, and shocked by her outfit, of course. But, they'd instantly embraced and welcomed her to their family. The photo opportunities had ensued. Her face had hurt. Her eyes had stung. Still, she'd posed with Alex and his family.

Now, she flexed her sore jaw as she dropped down onto the vanity seat in the empty ladies' room, thinking the attendant had taken a break. She sighed as she gazed at the tired look under her eyes.

Suddenly, the door blew open. Mrs. Royale sailed in. "Oh, there you are, my dear."

Charlie forced another smile as the older woman sank down beside her in the next seat.

"My, my," she said. Plucking a nearby tissue, she brushed it under her nose. "How sweet, isn't this all? Alex's parents would be so proud of him." She stopped and sniffled delicately. "Oh, don't mind me. Memories and all that."

"I'm sorry." She didn't know what else to say.

Mrs. Royale sucked in a deep breath. "I mustn't be sad, now. Why, I'm thrilled that Alex finally took the plunge. We'd been hoping he'd settle down for years." She leaned close, whispering, "It's better for business, you know."

A quiver of unease shot through Charlie's middle. "No, I didn't know that. How so?"

The older woman snapped open her tiny clutch and pulled out a tube of lipstick. "Why, he's more stable. There were some business opportunities that fell through because he was portrayed as such a playboy."

Charlie swallowed hard.

"And, of course, we had to be careful that no unsuitable girl got herself in the family way. There were accusations once."

This time Charlie's stomach lurched. "Really?"

"Gold digger." She pressed a hand to her mouth and looked up briefly. "Please, forgive me." Then she went right on talking. "She was only one of several. But this one, you see, her father wanted Royale Enterprises. He couldn't have it, or buy it, so he planned on his daughter sleeping with Alex. A few months later, she claims she's expecting." She whispered the last.

Charlie pressed a hand to her middle, suddenly feeling queasy. "Of course, she wasn't?"

Mrs. Royale waved her hand. "Oh, no, no. Thankfully not. Then there was the one, I think she was a few before that one. Well, her family's business was drowning in debt and, of all things, to rescue them, she tries to hook Alex. My goodness, what a mess that one was. She tried to sink Royale Enterprises to save their necks."

Looking at her own reflection, Charlie watched in horror as the blood drained from her face. "But," she licked her parched lips, "Royale Enterprises is fine now, right?"

It seemed to be the older woman's turn to turn pale. "Well," she hesitated, "I guess since you're family, you should know." She held up her thumb and forefinger an inch apart. "It's just a teensy-weensy bit, um, not at its best, if you know what I mean?"

She must have mumbled something.

"But Alex is going to fix it, just you wait and see. He's going to sew up that California deal." She shrugged. "Millions upon millions, you know? We'll have to move, make some adjustments-" She cleared her throat. "But, everything will be right as rain."

"Of course." It all made sense now. She was just like the others, expecting to salvage her company by marrying Alex.

But she'd assumed the marriage was to appease her stepmother and finally have the woman agree to the many changes to update King's. She'd had no idea her stepmother would bargain for her and in doing so, Alex would jeopardize his own business.

Guilt and shock warred in her middle.

The older woman babbled on about the guests, hinting at possible romances for her stepsisters. She even thought one of Alex's older, distinguished business associates had an eye for her stepmother.

Bile rose in her throat.

After applying the creamy, rose lipstick, the older woman drew her lips in and distributed the rich color. Next, she smiled widely, and then rubbed a finger over her teeth.

Once done, she turned to Charlie. "You know what the guests were saying before you arrived, my dear?" She reached out and poked Charlie's bare middle with her index finger. It wasn't quite a jab, but she felt it nonetheless. "That you and Alex had to marry. They said you were expecting. I guess you showed them, didn't you? Why, in an outfit like that, you'd never be able to disguise a little bump, now would you?"

Smiling weakly, Charlie forced herself not to throw up.

*   *   *

Charlie's head spun at the ongoing commotion.

The makeovers were a huge success, as she had predicted. But on the last day, she'd had enough of the constant female chattering, arguing over the best look for them, clothes tried on and discarded in a pile, and the whirl of people coming and going. Rico's occasional temper tantrums and Andre's hissy fits only added to the stress.

The bright lights and flashing cameras weren't helping the pounding in her temples. Before and after shots were necessities. But really, couldn't things calm down, even if it was just for a moment?

In the back of her mind, a fusion of fear snuck through. *Will it always be like this? One campaign after another? Will it ever be enough? Will I ever have time to just sit back and enjoy it all?* The questions nagged at her.

The one she didn't want to face reared its ugly head. When would she be able to design again? An ache of longing shot through her.

Sketching, dreaming up dress designs, had taken a back seat to all the other things she'd had to juggle recently.

"Holy Toledo, boss, call for you." Peg shoved the cell phone into her hand.

Instinctively, she grabbed for it and answered, "Charlotte King."

"You forgot the Royale," Alex reminded her.

"Alex, is that you?" *Of course it was, silly.* His voice eased the tension in her body.

"Unless you have another husband I don't know about."

She chuckled at his joke. "No. I can't seem to get the knack of this one yet." It came out more serious than she'd planned.

Silence reigned.

Mentally, she berated herself. "Sorry, that slipped out."

"I guess it's the truth for both of us, isn't it?" A tinge of sadness colored his words.

"Business."

"Family," he added.

Squeezing her eyes shut for a moment, Charlie said, "Obligations."

"Loyalty."

"Promises," she pointed out.

"Spoken and unspoken ones."

"Dreams." Her voice caught. "Fulfilled and unfulfilled." She thought of both their families' dreams.

"Theirs or ours?" He must have read her mind.

Another round of silence stretched for a long, uncomfortable moment.

"This is depressing," she said without thinking.

He chuckled. It came out strained. "Tell me about it."

She sighed.

"Look, I called to apologize."

Apologize, for what? The last time they'd seen each other he was making love to her. Slow, steady, wonderful, passionate love all night long after the party, she recalled dreamily. An ache, low and deep, curled through her. She wanted him. She wanted to touch his face, to look into his eyes again, and to feel his arms around her. He couldn't be sorry for their last night together, could he?

"I won't be able to make it today."

She shook off the wave of disappointment. "California calling?"

"Business in California calling, yes. I can't drag myself away. Important meetings."

Pressing past her hurt, she said, "Alex, you have to do this. Don't make it any harder for yourself than it has to be, all right? Believe me, I understand. I'm not going to be pulling you in one direction while your family and the business pull you in another. I don't want to do that to you," she said softly, blinking back tears. "I love you too much for that." Quickly, before he answered, she folded the cell phone shut, ending the call.

"Honey, what do you think?" Dolly asked as she waltzed out of the salon chair.

Focusing through the blur of tears, she spotted her friend. "Dolly!" She rushed up to her and gave her a quick, hard hug, and then pulled away. Gratitude at the diversion swept through her. "I can't believe the new you."

Gone were the curls and in its place was a smart, modern style with soft bangs and with slightly flipped-up layers. The gray had been replaced with a dark blonde shade with lighter highlights framing her face. "It brings out your eyes even more. And it makes your skin look radiant. Just beautiful."

Dolly giggled. "You think Eddie's gonna like it?"

"He'll love it."

"Good, cause we got a date tonight and I plan on some smoochie smoochie."

Chuckling, Charlotte hugged her friend again. This time a little longer and a little tighter. Thank goodness she had Dolly. She might be the only person she had left after all the dust cleared in a week or so.

Once she pulled away, Dolly eyed her closely. "You okay, sweetheart? You're losing too much weight and you look like you could collapse at any moment for the lack of sleep."

She brushed it off. "Long week. Too many campaigns so close together."

"Too much work for one body."

All she did was nod in agreement; she was too tired to talk.

"Well, you go take a break and I'll help out around here." She nudged Charlie's arm. "Look, even Francie and Prissy are lending a hand."

Her stepsisters had been here since an hour before the store opened and were more than willing to do anything asked of them.

"I'm grateful for your help and theirs."

They'd taken on some of the responsibilities, but ultimately she'd been conferred with for the last-minute details or glitches.

"Mayday, mayday, Charlie, come quick!" her assistant, Peg, cried from the doorway.

"Disaster?" she asked as she rushed to her, handing her back her phone.

"Holy Mamma Mia! Level four."

Groaning, she followed through the crowd of women at the makeup counter. "Fill me in as we go, Peg."

"Some woman has infiltrated the window display and is desperately trying to take your dress you wore at the party the grandparents threw for you and Alex. She thinks if she can look like you, she can get a man like yours."

This time Charlie cussed under her breath.

"Excuse me!" A nearby woman pulled back to look at her in horror.

"Fudge, ma'am. We're thinking of developing our own line of fudge and baked goodies to offer to our lovely customers." Pain shot through her cheeks at the effort it took her to paste on a phony grin.

The woman didn't seem convinced and, at the moment, Charlie didn't truly give a flying fig. She just wished this day would end and she could get some much needed rest.

Maybe it wouldn't have been so difficult if Alex could have made it. She sighed loudly.

He'd been gone all week long. The few phone calls hadn't been as impersonal as the first ones, but the bantering and warmth in his voice hadn't eased the ache in her heart.

The call she'd just hung up on made it so much worse. They both were highly aware of the problems they faced. She missed him terribly.

If what little bit of information she'd gathered this week were true, Alex would be spending more and more time away so he could focus on getting Royale Enterprises back on its feet and not be prey for a bigger company to swoop in for a takeover.

And with each day that passed, a sliver of reality sank in as well. The end was near for King's, for their employees, and for her hopes and dreams of keeping her father's legacy intact and thriving.

What would all of it do to Alex and her?

# CHAPTER 19

"You can drop me off here," Charlie said, leaning over the back seat to pay the taxicab driver.

"You sure, lady? I can bring you right to the doorstep."

She patted his shoulder. "No, thanks, I'll walk the last few yards."

He shrugged. "Whatever. Hey, thanks for the tip."

She barely heard the last as she shut the back door. He sped away. Standing on the corner, she gazed at the house she'd once called home. It didn't seem to harbor any wistful emotions this time. She walked the short distance, wondering when over the last few weeks she'd lost that connection.

This was her father's house. The house she'd grown up in with him, her mother, Dolly, and then her step-family. But, for once, she didn't long for everything to be turned back in time to relive those wonderful memories with him.

In a flash, she knew why. She'd found Alex. She'd found love.

Knocking on the door, she hoped her stepmother was home.

The big, wooden door opened effortlessly. A man she'd never met before looked down his nose. The short, older, perfectly groomed butler stood before her. "Yes?" His bored tone had Charlie biting her lip to keep from laughing.

Clearing her throat, she said, "Charlotte King to see Mrs. King, please."

He stretched out his long neck and raised his eyebrows, reminding her of a turtle. "Don't you mean Charlotte King Royale, ma'am?"

She bowed slightly. "Duly corrected, sir."

In the next few minutes, he ushered her into the foyer. She stood there until he could confirm if the mistress of the house was receiving any guests this evening.

While waiting, Charlie glanced around the big area. She never noticed how cold it seemed, even under all the faux gold. Her gaze landed on the doorway to the darkened dining room. That's where she'd met Alex, colliding into his arms. Had it only been a few weeks ago? She shook her head in wonder.

So much had changed. She had changed.

"Mrs. King will see you now."

Summoned, Charlie thought. She entered the parlor. The room hadn't changed a bit, but to Charlotte, she was a stranger viewing a familiar place.

"Charlotte, I'm surprised you would grace us with your presence. And on a Saturday night, at that!" Her stepmother's words were slightly slurred. She'd obviously been having a nip or two tonight.

"Yes, it's been quite some time." She didn't care to elaborate, so she changed the subject. "Did you enjoy the reception last week?"

She swore her stepmother's cheeks pinkened at the question. "Yes, yes."

*Nothing more to say, huh?* "I understand you met a gentleman there."

The older woman fidgeted with her pearl necklace. "I met several lovely people."

Refusing to be drawn into another charade, Charlie decided she'd ask what she came here to ask and be done with it. She sucked in a deep breath. "I've come to ask a favor, Stepmother."

"A favor?" She raised her brows and patted her neatly styled hair. "From me?"

*Yes, it was unheard of, wasn't it?* "I need you to stop the sale of King's—"

"Too late. It's done."

Her heart sank. She'd assumed as much, but tried anyway.

Her stepmother waved a hand in the air. "That was signed and completed weeks ago. Your husband has a team of crackerjack lawyers. They got things wrapped up rather quickly. At lightning speed, as a matter of fact. I'd imagine your husband would have mentioned that small detail to you by the way you grilled him when you found us in my office." If possible, her right eyebrow went even higher, nearly touching her hairline.

Certain her face would crack into tiny pieces if she attempted a smile, Charlie gathered her thoughts. "Can you buy it back?"

The older woman sputtered. "B-buy, it back?! Of all the ridiculous notions you've come up with over the years, Charlotte."

Desperation took hold and escalated. "What about my trust fund? Will you release it to me?"

The woman avoided looking at her. "No, of course not. You are not capable of handling that sum of money. Your father knew that."

For the first time she could recall, she grew angry with the man. "Why would he tie up my money with you?"

She made a noise in the back of her throat. "Charlotte King, who do you think created those trust funds and kept King's afloat for all these years? Me, that's who."

"The last twenty or so," she said aloud, "since Father died."

"Hah! Before that. Long before that. He was a great salesman, a genius when it came to people. Why they just fell in love with him the moment they met him-same thing with you."

"Me?" All she could do was blink at this woman who'd given her a compliment. Back-handed, but a compliment nonetheless, she noted.

Her stepmother rose and went to the drink cabinet. "Any for you?"

She pressed her hand to her flip-flopping belly. "No, thank you."

The woman gulped back one and poured the next. Turning toward Charlie, she said, "Yes, you have that same charisma as your father did. I worked for him, in the accounting department, soon after he opened the store."

Charlotte never knew that fact.

"Oh, what a charmer. He made everyone feel as if he was only interested in them." She sat down beside Charlie and visibly shivered. "Electricity."

"I'm not sure I need to hear this part," Charlie chimed in, not wanting to see that visual.

"I was young, impressionable. I thought he'd leave your mother for me."

Charlie sucked in a sharp breath.

The older woman reached out and touched her arm uncomfortably, and then drew back. "I didn't steal him. I left King's. Business was booming then. But a few years later, after you were born, and your mother was dying, he was beside himself. Doctor after doctor, bills after bills. He would have done anything for her." She choked out the last. "The company was near bankruptcy."

"No," Charlie gasped, stunned at the insight.

"He may have watched his pennies as you girls like to say, but if there are no pennies, then there's nothing to watch, is there?" She gazed down at the amber liquid in her glass. "I'd already been married, had the girls, and was no longer married. Your father asked me to come back. He needed me to help him with the business."

"So you went."

She sighed heavily. "Yes. Soon after your mother passed away. That's all he had left. You and King's. He held on dear to both. And I," she bit her lip, "I was relentless in comforting him."

The news didn't surprise her at all. Her stepmother was ruthless when she wanted something.

Getting up from the sofa, the older woman turned away sharply. "I loved him," she said without a hint of excuse in her tone. "I built up that company by his side. I was the one who saved it then. I brought it back from the brink."

Confused, Charlie asked, "So why refuse these last few years? Didn't you want to see it thrive? We could still do it. Time is still on our side." She stopped just short of begging.

Her stepmother whirled around. "Well, time is not still on *my* side. I want a life. For once I want what I want, not someone else's dream. King's Department

Store died a long time ago, Charlotte; you refuse to see that fact."

If she'd had a dagger, it couldn't have cut Charlie to the quick any faster than her words had. "Then let me do it. My trust fund—"

"Isn't enough."

"What about mine?" Francine asked, coming into the room.

Priscilla was close on her heels. "And mine."

"Girls!" Their mother's shocked voice reverberated in the room.

Charlotte stood and went to her stepsisters, hugging both of them. When she released them, she said, "Thank you, but I can't ask you to do it."

"You're not and we want to," Priscilla said matter-of-factly.

"Over my dead body," the older woman warned, gaining their full attention. "Absolutely not. I will have complete control of your trust funds, even after I die; it's in my will."

"Mother!" Francine's horror-filled voice seemed to echo all of their feelings.

"But, but," Priscilla sputtered. "You swore we could do what we wanted with it. After we're thirty."

Her eyebrow rose again and her lips became even more pinched. "I lied."

The gasps that surrounded Charlie caused her to reach out and grab hold of her swaying stepsisters. The truth was too ugly to bear.

"Why, Mother? Why would you say such a thing when it wasn't true?"

The older woman refused to answer.

"Why the trust funds, then? Why create them when you had no intention of honoring them?" Charlie asked in confusion. A wave of understanding took hold. "Father would never have allowed you to have all the money after he died. So you convinced him this was for the best. He agreed. You're the executrix. You get paid for maintaining them."

"And don't forget she doesn't have to pay taxes on the money this way either," Priscilla chimed in.

Charlie continued, "Yes, the girls get an allowance —"

"A pittance," Francie pointed out.

"You, Stepmother, manipulated everything." Charlie's words tumbled out as the thoughts rushed in her mind. "And still do."

This time, the woman seemed to shrink right before their very eyes. She sank down into a nearby chair. Tears welled. "I had to keep you close." She waved a hand in Charlie's direction. "I knew she'd never accept me. I didn't care, not as long as I still had you two."

"So you controlled their every move by dangling the money over their heads," Charlie said softly, cringing at that.

Feeling her stepsisters shake, she gently led them to the sofa to sit. She planted herself between the pair.

Grasping their hands, she asked, "And what about marrying them off?"

Waving at them as if to dismiss that question, she said, "I'll choose the husbands they need. Rich, yet malleable. In the meantime, I'll still have them to do as I say and I'll be able to arrange their marriages to my liking. And to top it all off, once they're married or by the time they're thirty, I'll have more control of the bulk of the funds. Why else would I hunt for spouses for them now?"

"Dictate to them and their husbands to get your hands on the money?" Even Charlie had a difficult time believing the absurdity of that concept.

"But Alex won't allow that," Priscilla pointed out.

"No," her mother sighed heavily, "but then I could never control Charlotte, now could I?" She halted for a moment. "That's why she doesn't have a trust fund."

"What?!" Charlie and her sisters asked in unison.

"Nothing. Not a dime for you, Charlotte King."

Charlie felt the color drain from her face. Her stepmother tricked her father and now her. Did her stepmother hate her that much? Or did she love money more?

"It's her family's money," Francie protested.

Dawning hit Charlie then. "That's why you agreed to my marriage to Alex. There was no trust fund, but he was rich. Rich enough to buy the store. You really did sell me off."

"The girls had no prospects in sight. So, yes, he did have the money I needed to retire."

"Royale Enterprises, you mean," Charlie muttered under her breath.

Beside her, Francine shook even more. "Mother, how could you do this to Charlie, to us? You treat us nothing like real women. We have thoughts, ideas—"

"Feelings," Priscilla added.

"Hopes and dreams," Charlie tacked on.

"You?" the older woman snapped back. "Hah! You're so busy trying to chase a dead man's dreams. Far-fetched, ridiculous dreams, he couldn't even achieve. You think I have no life? Well, look at your own, Charlotte. You had nothing but back-breaking day in and day out work before I stepped in and arranged your marriage. Now, at least you have a future."

Charlie saw clearly now. There was some truth in what the woman said. Her stepmother's crushed hopes, sense of rejection, loneliness, anger, hurt, greed, and jealousy all clung to her like a second skin. She paid the highest price of all. Love.

She'd never had the love she'd wanted. No, she'd had to compete with King's Department Store, her father's obsession with making it a success, her mother, Charlotte, and even her own two daughters.

With this new discovery, Charlotte gazed long and hard at her stepmother. She saw herself in thirty years. Oh, maybe not the bitter, cold woman sitting across from her, but the loss of herself. For what? Pushing people away? The drive, the ambition, and the success? Money? Would they be her only companions late at night? Would she always sacrifice herself?

*A secondhand life?* Is that what she wanted for herself?

A cold shiver raked her body.

Francine stood. On shaky legs, Charlie joined her and so did Priscilla. "I won't stand for this a moment longer." She turned to Charlie. "Do you still have your apartment? You haven't sublet it yet, have you?"

"No, it's still available."

"We'll take it," Priscilla said, strength growing in her voice.

Charlie could only imagine the two women in a cramped loft.

"I won't let you," their mother exclaimed.

"You can't stop us." Francine, with fisted hands on her hips, faced her mother.

"You have no money. Your disobedience warrants me to discontinue your allowance. It's in the will."

"You'll cut us off? So be it," Priscilla said, folding her arms over her chest. "I would rather be broke than living the miserable life you've created for us. Piano lessons, please! I stink at the piano. And I hate wearing black dresses all the time."

Francine said, "Well, it's going to be easy to pack, now won't it?"

Less than an hour later, Charlotte and her stepsisters, dragging a suitcase each, closed the door behind them.

In the background, she could still hear her stepmother shouting, "Girls, girls! I demand you stop this nonsense immediately."

Climbing into the back of the awaiting taxicab, Charlotte turned to each one. "Are you sure about this?" She was certain there was no turning back now.

"Hell, yes!" the twosome shouted with joy.

Charlie was afraid of that. Just what in the world was she doing? For all intents and purposes, the girls needed tutoring. Living independently didn't come naturally to women who were used to be taken care of all their lives. And Charlie knew she would be the one to assist them. Some example she'd be. How could she help them when she couldn't even save herself or, most likely, her marriage?

# CHAPTER 20

Much later that night, in the shadowed store, Charlie wandered through each department, lovingly trailing her hands over the display cases. In the linen department, she sunk down on the edge of the perfectly made double bed and rested her face in her hands, her elbows digging into her knees.

"All this," she whispered, "will be gone in just a few days." Six weeks had flown by and now it was time to face facts. "The cold, hard facts." Tears smarted her eyes. "King's no more."

"Miss Charlie, that you? You all right?" Bruno's voice yanked her from her pity party.

She sat up, dropping her hands to her lap. "No date for you?"

"Wife's out with the girls tonight." He pointed to a spot by her. "Mind?"

She shook her head. "Nope. Pull up a seat and sit a spell, my friend."

He dropped down, his weight shifting the bed. Their shoulders bumped briefly. He let out a heavy sigh.

"Tired?"

"And then some."

She hated to see him like this. "I thought you were going to retire a few years back."

"Ah, you know, I can't seem to let go of this place."

Swallowing hard, she looked away from him. "Me neither."

"Lots of people here like that. A lot of the old-timers could've retired a while back, but decided to stay on. Gets in their blood, you know." He laughed at himself. "Well, it is in your blood."

She chuckled, but there was a sad edge to it. Then she recalled their devotion to her. "I don't want all of you staying because of me."

He ducked his head in embarrassment. "Oh, well, you know, your daddy always asked us to look out for you."

"I was a kid then, coming and going from the store." Working, pitching in whenever and wherever she could, she recalled.

"We sorta took it upon ourselves after he passed."

This time she swiped at a fast falling tear. "Family."

"The King's family," he corrected; his chest seemed to puff up. "Loyal to the core."

"Maybe that's a problem."

"Huh?"

She blew out a hot breath. "Someday this place may not be here." *Sooner than you know, my friend.*

"We were afraid that might happen."

"You all know?"

He took off his hat and scratched his head, and then replaced it. "It's not a secret. Never has been. But you, these few weeks, breathing new life back in the store, well, it gave us some hope."

"Hope." She said that one word. Had she lost it all? Had she given King's employees false hope and just delayed the inevitable? Was she doing that with Alex, too?

\*\*\*

"We're here, sir," Edward pointed out unnecessarily as he put the car in park.

Alex nodded, but kept staring out of the side window. He took in the window displays. The first one bore the re-creation of Charlie and him dancing intimately at the party. He sucked in a sharp breath, remembering the feel of her in his arms, then and much later. His body tightened. He fought off the wave of desire.

Blowing out a hot breath, he focused on the second window. A smile tugged at the corner of his mouth. Charlie, in her skimpy business attire, was splayed out in her chair behind her desk littered with papers and drawings. He, dressed in a stiff, navy blue suit, stood nearby flipping through a file.

Both figures were obviously overwhelmed by their jobs. The truth of it probably poked at many a couple. How could you work full-time yet keep a marriage going and in two different cities?

He would definitely like the answer to that one.

"This is it." He yanked on the handle and shoved the door open. "Wish me luck, my friend."

"Yeah, right," Edward muttered loud enough for Alex to hear.

In less than twenty minutes, he'd effortlessly met the guard, had been ushered in, and had been whisked up the elevator to the executive's offices.

As he walked to Charlie's office, his heart pounded. For a Sunday afternoon, no one occupied the floor. Was she even here? Dolly had relayed that message to Edward.

Her office, holding her essence, was empty. He lingered for a few moments, taking it all in, taking in the part of her he may never see again.

Reluctantly, he turned and retraced his steps. At the receptionist desk, he moved down the aisle toward the stepmother's old office. Surely she wouldn't be there? But he heard a noise to his right and stopped at the doorway.

Charlie was there, sitting at the head of the conference table with her palms resting on the rich, cherry wood. Apparently lost in thought, she didn't know he was there.

Swallowing hard, he tapped on the door. She jerked her head toward him. She pressed a hand to her chest. "Alex, you scared me. I didn't realize you were coming home today."

Her eyes remained guarded as he entered the room. "Just for today. Dinner with my grandparents then I'm off to California again tomorrow morning." He wanted to include her, but reasoned after what he was about to say, she wouldn't want much to do with him any longer. Something sharp and heavy kicked him in his gut. He clamped down on his growing sense of despair.

She bit her lip. He longed to go to her and kiss away her worry. But he couldn't. He couldn't even ease his own mind. Not about this decision.

He came as close as he dared, and then rested a hip on the sleek, wooden table. As he settled down, he noticed how she now gripped the edge of the table, her knuckles turning white. Guilt jabbed him.

"I'll get this over with as fast as possible," he said, thinking the quicker he said this, the better.

She paled considerably. "By all means." He didn't even see her lips move.

Digging into the inside pocket of his jacket, he withdrew a thick, creamy white business envelope. He gazed at it. Regret tugged at him, yet it had been the only answer he'd come up with in the end.

He hesitated, gripping the paper for a moment longer. Sighing heavily, he slid the envelope across the table. It glided to her. She reached out and stopped it from going over the edge.

"And this is?" He heard the quiver in her voice.

The muscle in his jaw jumped as he clenched his teeth together. God, he didn't think he'd ever hurt this much again. "King's." He dropped the one word into the air like a bomb.

She visibly gulped. "You've sold it then?"

"Royale Enterprises sold it. They are no longer the owners of King's Department Store."

She clutched the envelope beneath her hand, wrinkling it. "Who is?"

He had to word this just so. "The store was sold, then it was gifted to someone."

Shock chased across her features. "What are you hiding, Alex? Tell me."

"I bought the store, Charlotte."

She seemed to wince at the use of her full name. "You? How? Why?"

He let out a breath, trying to stop his head from spinning. *This can't be happening.* "Let's just say I had some holdings I liquidated."

Anger flashed in her eyes. "Holdings? Shares? Stocks? What exactly are we talking about?"

He raised an eyebrow. Inwardly, he loved her feistiness. "That's not important."

"It is to me—" She stopped herself in mid-sentence, quickly rising from her chair. "No, Alex," she shook her head, "not that."

*What did she suspect?*

"The island house!"

*And the island. And the yacht.* She knew. He grimaced. "It's mine to do with what I want."

"But the papers said it's the one you love the most."

*No, you are.*

She clamped her eyes shut. When she opened them again, her hurt gaze captured his stare. "Turquoise. When you told me it was your favorite color, you were talking about the island water."

He could only nod at the documents she was grasping in both hands.

"It went for a tidy sum and pushed the amount over the top. I don't know why I didn't think of it before."

"No, you can't. I won't let you," she insisted, holding out the envelope to him.

He glanced at it, and then back at her. "Too late. It's done. Those papers are yours."

She frowned. "Mine? I don't understand."

"That, my dear, is the gift part. I'm giving you back your precious King's."

*Charlie gets her store. Royale Enterprises gets millions from the sale, safe for now from a takeover. And my grandparents' peace of mind is back. Everything and everyone I care about is safe and sound.*

He halted for a moment, knowing he had to say the next, but not wanting to. He nearly choked on the next words. "It's part of the divorce settlement."

Sinking back in the chair, Charlie's face drained of all color. His heart squeezed in his chest. How in the world could he walk away from her? He had no choice.

"Divorce?!" The questions swam in her eyes but she couldn't seem to voice any.

"Business," he said, too sharply, feeling the all too powerful obligation to his family. "I'll be relocating to California. Two years of developing the biggest and most ambitious Royale Enterprises project ever." The deal was finalized. His grandfather was thrilled at the news, knowing the company would thrive.

Alex waved a hand to encompass the room. "You'll be here running your family business. I'll be there running my family business. There's no room for a long-distance marriage, Charlie." This time he couldn't bear to be harsh with her. His heart ached.

"What about the great-grandchild, Alex? Your grandparents still want that."

He loved the fight in her. She wasn't letting go easily. But, he had to, for both of their sakes. "A child needs both parents, Charlie; we both know that. *We* needed both our parents. We didn't get that lucky, did we?" He swallowed hard. "I can't do that to a child - not now, maybe ever."

"Marriage and," she bit her lip, "well, it just won't fit in the business plans, will it? Once, not so long ago, you thought it could."

"That was before I met you," he choked out, and then went on, "*Family* business plans." *Theirs, not mine. I owe that to them.*

"Family first, right?" she asked. Her chin quivered.

"If you think about it, Charlie, we've both been after the same goal."

Confusion furrowed her brow.

"You are trying to keep King's Department Store up and running. Is it for the sake of the store itself?" He shook his head. "I don't think so. You, my dear, are trying to resurrect a man who died years ago. You're trying to keep your father alive."

Stunned wonder washed over her face. "And you?"

"I, well, I'm trying to literally keep my grandparents alive by keeping their dreams intact of Royale Enterprises and all it can become."

"Holding on—"

"Yes." He stopped for a moment, and then revealed a secret he'd been guarding for years. "I promised my dying parents I would."

"What?"

"They survived the plane crash, Charlie, briefly. I've never told anyone, except Edward."

"Not even your grandparents?"

"No, it would have hurt them too much to have them think my parents suffered."

"But you were only a boy. The burden you had to carry."

He closed his eyes for a moment, in awe that she could see how difficult it had been. "They begged me to take care of my grandparents."

"You gave your word."

"Yes."

"And no one should break their word. Your word is your honor."

"You remember."

"I'll never forget." This time she turned away from him, not able to hold his stare.

\*\*\*

Later, after Alex had walked away and out of her life, Charlie made it back to her office on shaky legs. Her head spun, her middle clenched, and her body grew clammy. Leaning on the desk, she drew in great, big gulps of air.

With tunnel vision, everything narrowed. Charlie stared down at the thick envelope she'd placed on her father's desk. It was right there in black and white.

She had all she'd ever wanted. King's Department Store was now hers. So why wasn't she ecstatic over the fact?

*Have you ever gotten all you ever wanted, then, once you had it, you realized you may not want it anymore?*

She had no idea how long she was there before she heard Dolly's voice, and then her stepsisters.

"Honey, are you all right?" The warm, comforting hand of her friend rested on her back. "Eddie called, said to come quick you needed me. Why, me and the girls hustled right over here."

A smile tugged at her stiff lips. Yes, she could always count on Dolly. Her stomach rolled. She pressed a hand to her middle.

"I'm going to be sick," she announced as she rushed from the room, out of Peg's office and to the executive bathrooms. The door banged against the wall as she made it just in time.

Behind her, she heard Priscilla. "Gross. What did you eat anyway?"

"She ain't been hardly eating at all," Dolly pointed out.

"I'll get some wet paper towels for you, Charlie," Francine offered.

With her belly empty at last, Charlie flushed. Gratefully, she grabbed for the damp towels, pressing them to her forehead, face, and then neck. "I have to rinse," she said.

With her sisters helping her to the sinks and Dolly holding her up from the back, Charlie reached for the faucet. Twisting the cold knob to full blast, she stuck her mouth under it. She swished and then spit. After a few more tries at that, she came up for air.

One sister leaned over to turn off the knob. The other handed over fresh paper towels. Dolly clucked in sympathy.

Charlie caught a glimpse of her reflection. Pale with dark circles under her eyes and hollow cheeks, she barely recognized herself.

"I have definitely gone to the dogs," she muttered, seeing the dark pools of her eyes. Maybe it was shock. After all, less than two months of marriage and her husband had just left her.

"You're working too hard." Priscilla patted her on the forearm.

"She is at that," Francine agreed.

"Either that or she's pregnant," Dolly said offhandedly.

Charlie froze. The others followed suit as they met her shocked gaze in the mirror. With as much effort as she could, she shook her head. "It can't be."

"Aren't you two, ah, close?" Priscilla asked hesitantly.

Her cheeks turned pink, giving her some color at last. "Prissy!"

"Well, are you?" Francine challenged.

"Of course they are." Dolly tsked them all.

"Dolly, do you have to advertise the fact?" Charlie looked at her with wide, questioning eyes.

"It ain't no secret, honey. Why, you and Mr. R. got a healthy, real healthy—"

"All right, you don't have to go there," Charlie interrupted.

"You're expecting," Dolly said with a growing smile, "that's the only answer."

"No, it's not."

"Is, too," the girls chimed in.

"Quit, all three of you." Charlie gulped hard.

"We'll end this once and for all." Dolly nodded. "You girls go get a pregnancy test."

"Us?" they shrieked in unison.

The older woman dug out some money from the bosom of her dress. "Here, take this and run on down to the drugstore. While you're at it, get a toothbrush and toothpaste, too."

"I can't be," Charlie said over and over again as she paced the small, cramped bathroom, waiting for the girls to return from their errand.

Dolly watched, smiling brightly. "We'll just see about that, missy."

Much later, while counting the seconds for the results, Charlie repeated, "I can't be."

"It's time," Francine announced.

Charlie turned to the stick, and then swallowed hard.

"Well, go ahead and get it. We wanna see, too." Dolly's hand nudged her back.

Gingerly, she carried it to the well-lit sink area, avoiding looking directly at the indicator.

As the others crowded close to her, hemming her in, she muttered, "Well, here goes nothing. Or everything."

# CHAPTER 21

Charlie hadn't come home last night. Worry had plagued Alex. But he had it on good authority that Dolly was with her. Her friend would comfort her and take good care of her; that he could guarantee.

"But she shouldn't have to," he said under his breath.

"Sir?"

He waved off his friend. "Oh, nothing, Edward." For the first time, he realized his driver wasn't en route to the airport. "Where are we going?" he asked much too sharply.

"King's."

He frowned, his middle dipping. "And why is that?"

Edward shrugged. "Orders, sir."

"From who? And I thought you were working for me."

His grin filled the reflection in the rearview mirror. "Dolly, that's who from. And, as far as I know, I still work for you."

Alex shook his head. But then a thought came. "Is it Charlie? Is she all right?"

"Well, it's not an emergency or anything." Edward seemed to debate over his answer.

"You're keeping a secret from me?"

"Not entirely, sir," he said. "I don't know a lot, just what Dolly wants to tell me. But, from what she says, it's for your own good, let me just say that."

"That is not saying much," he complained.

He kept silent after that, mulling over the reason for his delay. For all he knew, Charlie might be just as much in the dark about this as he was. Charlie. Just the thought of her had him tied up in knots.

When his grandfather had insisted on Alex having dinner with the all-female King family, he'd had no idea how much his life would be turned upside down. But it had and he welcomed the all too brief time with his wife.

Charlie. The sight of her. Her scent, light and heavenly. Her smile. Those dark, luminous eyes. Her humor. She made him laugh more in the last few weeks than he could ever recall doing in his entire life. He ached for her.

He would never forget her.

"So did you ever ask your grandfather about creating a West Coast division?" Edward asked.

"Are you just trying to make conversation?"

"Beats worrying, doesn't it?"

"Something like that," Alex countered, using Charlie's phrase. He heaved a heavy sigh. "He wasn't that receptive to the idea. Expenses, overhead, finding quality staff. No, Dallas will always be home base. He and Grandmother are already counting on the sun and fun the next two years."

"I can't see them being uprooted from all they're familiar with, do you?"

No, he couldn't either. How could two elderly people, cut off from all they were familiar with, leave their hometown after sixty years of marriage and more than forty years of that living in the same home? They loved their home, their friends, their longtime doctors, the clubs they belonged to, and especially the parties his grandmother adored throwing for the people she cared for the most.

Another thought nudged his conscience. They would give up everything for him. And they had once before. "Do you think they're just saying that? You know, for the business and to be close to me still?"

"Seems so, if you don't mind me saying."

"Edward, when have I had a choice in what you say?" He chuckled, taking the sting out of the question.

"That's true. Lucky for me."

Alex leaned forward, patting him on the shoulder, saying, "No, lucky for me, friend, lucky for me." He thanked whoever every day for placing Edward in his life.

Who would have thought an ex-cop with a bum knee would have dragged him out of a bar that night in college and saved him from untold scandal? He couldn't convince his friends and they'd ended up being arrested. The incident, and the subsequent discovery of illegal activities at the nightclub, had made the papers for months. Guilt by association and jail time ensued.

In saving Alex's neck and the Royale family reputation, Edward had made a friend for life. So had Alex.

"Maybe it's time to expand into an uncharted market for Royale Enterprises. If we coincide this with the new development, we assure the client undivided attention and spotlight their build in our publicity campaign. Both companies win, free advertising for them while we cultivate more projects in the process. West Coast division needs a West Coast chief," he mused. "Chadwick would love the opportunity."

Edward laughed. "Perfect. Gets him out of your hair."

"And gets him the prestige he wants."

"He'll be happier."

"Yes and he will be less likely to defect to another company, taking all that knowledge and expertise he has with him. He'd sign that contract without a second thought. His loyalty to the company all these years should be rewarded. Charlie would think so, too. And the man deserves a bonus for all his hard work. An all-expense paid vacation with his family, I think. Royale

Enterprises would benefit greatly by allowing him to head up his own division." Alex spoke his thoughts out loud.

"And you get to stay put," Edward ended with a hopeful note to his voice.

For the first time, Alex realized Edward would have to give up Dolly, too. It just wasn't Alex losing what he cared about most.

"Family first, Edward, that's what she said."

"Miss Charlie? She's a smart one."

Edward was just as much family to him as Dolly was to Charlie. He pictured King's employees. Their dedication and devotion were not just to a store, but to the Kings themselves. Charlie always said the employees were members of King's family.

And Charlie was part of *his* family now.

Alex's heart lurched.

He'd married in order to save his grandparents. His mission was to keep them and their hope alive. But, in finding Charlie, she'd been the one to rescue *his* secret hope of ever having a future filled with love and family.

He could have everything he ever longed for with Charlie. He couldn't lose her now.

"We're here, sir."

Alex came out of his reverie with a start. Without thinking, he got out of the car. He made it a few steps and then halted, looking at the new window display.

"Sir, you all right?" Edward asked, now at his elbow.

"How could I have forgotten? I took a vow, Edward. I gave my word." *Love, honor, and cherish.*

"And you always keep your word, sir."

Moving closer, he felt his friend right by his side. There, behind the glass, stood the mannequins. Charlie, with Dolly and the stepsisters by her side, was in a makeshift bathroom, staring at something Charlie was holding. It was too small to see.

He read the title under the Charmings. *A baby makes three?*

"It can't be."

"That's what she said," Dolly exclaimed, having come up to him.

He gazed at her in stunned wonder. "Well, is she or isn't she?"

The older woman tapped a finger against her lips. "Mums the word, Mr. R." She pointed a thumb over her shoulder, saying, "But you'll find your answer over there."

He rushed past her. Finding the window drape still covering the second display, he turned back to find Dolly with Edward at her side. She then nodded to the stepsister at the entrance to King's.

"Hit it, Francine," Priscilla cried out.

The drape moved. He struggled to make out the images behind the fabric. Slowly, the material parted, revealing the scene.

Time seemed to slow. Blood rushed to his ears.

Right before his eyes, blue and pink linens littered the area. With only half his mind working, he noticed the white wooden crib, rocker, and matching furniture. Resting on top of a large blue pillow was a miniature jewel-encrusted crown and beside it, on the matching pink pillow, was a miniature diamond tiara.

"Congratulations, Alex, you're going to be a daddy." Charlie's sweet voice came from his left.

Whirling around, he saw her standing just a few steps away.

Alex drank in the sight of her. He could never get enough of seeing her wide smile and sparkling eyes filled with love.

He found home.

His heart hitched in his chest.

And, he noted, she was carrying those strappy red shoes again. "What is it with you and the shoes?" he joked, turning the familiar question around on her.

She giggled. "If the shoe fits, isn't that what you said the first time we met? I thought they came with the prince."

"If you remember correctly, you had the shoes before me."

"Of course, how could I forget? You, Alexander Royale, were the icing on the cake."

Sobering, he waved a hand to the second window display. "Charlie, you're serious, aren't you?"

"Of course, silly, I would never pull a prank like this. It's true." She bit her lip. "Alex, I don't want King's anymore. I'm going to hand it over to the employees. It's their store, really. Their hard work and dedication has made it into what it is today. They can decide if they want to keep it going or not. If they sell the place, they'll have a pretty profit for retirement or whatever else they wish to do with the money."

"But, Charlie, this is your life."

She shook her head. "It's not. You were right. I was trying to hold onto my father. It's not fair to try to keep a ghost alive. Not to him, and especially not to us. I can't live someone else's dream anymore. I have to live my own. You, Alex, well, you and the baby," she touched her flat belly, "you're now my life."

She stole his breath away. "I'm the luckiest guy in the world," he said softly, overcome with emotions. "I want to hold you in my arms forever."

"I want that, too."

"That's a relief."

"You have to have big arms," she pointed out.

"For you?"

She shrugged. "Me, the baby, Dolly, Francine, Priscilla—"

"The shoes," he teased.

"Just the red ones."

"Your stepmother?" he asked with a hint of dismay.

"Not yet." She sighed. "Eventually though. Can you handle that?"

He grinned. "Is that all you got?"

"More babies?"

"Definitely. Plus my grandparents and Edward. That's a pretty good life, the way I see it."

"The best. Not too shabby for a King and a Royale."

He walked to her then. He brushed back a lock of her hair and cupped her cheek. "But you love what you do. You can't give that up."

"Oh, I didn't say I was throwing in the towel on everything. I think with my dress designs, Dolly's skills, and my sisters as my two new assistants, we can get our new company up and running soon. We can sell the line exclusively at King's if it's still open."

"A King will still be a part of King's Department Store. They'll be lucky to have you."

"I thought of a name for the new business: *Charmed, I'm Sure.*"

"You are amazing."

"Of course I am. Either here or in California. Bi-coastal or whatever you call it."

He chuckled. "I don't think that will be necessary. The deal is sealed. There's no backing out now. And as top dog of Royale Enterprises, I think it's high time I make an executive decision to open up a West Coast division. I know the perfect candidate to fill the chief position."

"But your grandparents?"

"They'll be too busy with their new great-grand—" he stopped himself. "Boy or girl?"

"I betcha it will be one of those two."

"I thought you never bet on a sure thing?"

"Except when it comes to ice cream tasting."

"Or cards," he pointed out with a smile in his voice, recalling the all-aces, all-hearts deck.

"That, my love, was betting on you, not the cards," she whispered huskily.

Warmth spread through him. She was going to have his baby. Another thought tugged at him. "Does this mean I still have to court you?"

"For a lifetime, husband."

"My pleasure, wife."

She dropped the shoes. Charlie threw her arms around him and kissed him. Alex held her close, returning her deep, lingering kiss.

He heard Edward, Dolly, and Charlie's stepsisters clap and cheer.

In the back of his mind, Alex realized, the Charmings would be living happily ever after after all.

Now, if they could just marry off the stepsisters…

**The End**

Here's an excerpt from Waking Sleeping Beauty, Book 2 in the Once Upon A Romance Series.

## WAKING SLEEPING BEAUTY

## CHAPTER 1

"Wake up, will ya!"

Francine King bolted upright in the tiny enclosure. She blinked several times, trying to recall where she was. Looking down at the layers of satin and lace dress with hundreds of tiny crystals sparkling under the lights, she landed back to earth with a dull thud. "Rico?"

"Of course, it's me, silly. Who else would it be?"

She sighed with relief. "Sorry. I'm just jumpy."

"And sleepy," he muttered. "No rest for the new independent woman, now is there?"

"Did you get them?" She stood, sweeping layers of fabric in a neater array. "I'm decent. You can come in now."

He shoved aside the curtain to the dressing room and produced the two carat, teardrop diamond earrings. "Viola." He swung the sparkling pair under her nose.

"Do I deliver or do I de-" he stopped in midstream, his mouth hanging open. "Shut up!"

Heat crawled into her cheeks. Pressing her hands to her face, she asked, "Is that a good shut up or a bad shut up?"

"O-M-G! You look fab-u-loicous, girl." His eyes nearly popped out of his head.

"I take that as good." She smiled now, fingering the delicate lace bodice on the wedding dress. "It's not too much. Or should I say too little?" she asked, splaying her hand over the deep V neckline.

"You have bubbies."

Another sweep of heat seared her cheeks. "You sound like that's a question, not a statement." Looking down, she noted the miraculous way the dress pushed her together to create a definite cleavage.

"Come out, come out. Let me see more."

Poking her head out of the dressing room, she looked down the aisle. "Is the coast clear?"

"Everyone's gone for the night or we wouldn't be here, you know that."

"No one followed you? No guards? No manager? You know she doesn't like me."

He sighed heavily. "Now who does?"

A stab of hurt lanced through her. "Rico!"

Pursing his lips together, he murmured, "It's true."

This time she was the one to sigh. She marched out of the cubicle, down the hallway and into the display room. Her so-called new friend didn't mince words and she'd be forever grateful for that. But the truth did hurt. She stepped up onto the pedestal and gazed unseeingly into her reflection in the full length mirror opposite her.

"Here, let me do the back up all the way," he clucked, delicately handing over the precious jewelry. He tugged at the satin strings, pulling the wedding dress even tighter.

"I didn't do anything," she whispered, slipping on the earrings. "I'm not my mother. I'm not mean or vain or pushy-"

"Well…" He coughed a few times. "You can be pushy, but, like me, it's for a good cause. You're just trying to help out around the store." He waved a hand. "Helping the salespeople with their customers. I swear some people don't have a lick of common sense when dealing with the public."

She forced herself to grin. "Not like us, right?" Being a hairdresser in King's Department Store salon allowed Rico to judge the wisdom of his clients' choices. He expressed his opinion on more than just hair and makeup and clothes. Nine times out of ten, he nailed it on the head.

And she, the stepdaughter to the late, great Charles King, enjoyed the breath of fresh air Rico brought to the legendary store. Taking a cue from him, she didn't hold back on her suggestions for the brides who shopped there. After all, if anyone knew about weddings, she did. Francine lived and breathed weddings. She considered herself an amateur expert on the subject; she poured over bridal magazines and collected pictures in her three-ring wedding binder for decades now. Her heart skipped a beat at the thought of her dream wedding.

Only there were a few things wrong with the picture.

Even after all these years, she still couldn't decide on a dress. She couldn't have a perfect wedding without the perfect wedding dress, now could she?

She'd never be able to afford her picturesque day now that her mother had cut off her trust fund. How long would it take to save for the lavish affair? Two years? Three? More?

And last, but not least, she faced another even larger dilemma.

It was just too bad she'd never dated anyone in her entire life.

No groom. Now that could be a big sticking point.

"Francie, don't slouch." He smacked her lightly on her bottom.

She sucked in a breath and twirled to him.

"It was just a pat," he soothed. "Pay attention. Now turn around and behave."

Folding her arms over her chest, she asked, "Me?"

"Look, face it. You're not Miss Popularity around here. That award goes to Charlie."

She should be offended, but she wasn't. She smiled now. Her older stepsister was the heir apparent and had worked in the store for years, gaining the love and trust of the employees. Francie and her younger sister, Priscilla, had only joined King's a few weeks ago when they'd abruptly walked out on their demanding, controlling mother. Her smile faded quickly at the thought of the woman who'd she'd never really known, but she had listened to and blindly obeyed all these years.

"I know, Rico, it's not that. They brand me with the same brush they use for my mother," she choked out the last.

He shivered in revulsion. "No offense, but that woman gives me the willies. Just one look from her and she'd knock off her enemy. Thank God she's greedy and sold off the store to your new brother-in-law."

"At least Charlie and he saved the store from closing."

"Ah, I hear it ain't a sure thing."

"What?!" Immersed in trying to stand on her own two feet, working long extra hours to just survive and keep a stern watch over her younger sister, Francie hadn't the time to sit down with Charlie to discuss the store's numbers.

"The holidays will either make or break the store."

Her heart sank. Fear slithered in, cold and dark. What in the world would her family do if the store closed? This was her stepfather's dream. Charlie had kept it going with her brilliant ad campaigns lately. And she and Priscilla were not adept at anything, not even being a salesperson. They'd only gotten their jobs at the store thanks to Charlie and being family.

"Quit frowning. Look, all done up." He stood back. "Lovely."

Jerked back to the moment, Francie came to attention. She fingered her blonde bob into place, then, not liking the look, pulled her hair up off her neck. "Better, don't you think?"

"Much," he agreed.

Suddenly, the lights flickered off and on and off and on again.

"Oh no, that's the guards, the last warning for the employees."

Rico jumped. "Oh my God, I've got to get the earrings back in the vault."

"You took them from the vault?"

"I figured you could use some bling when you tried on the latest arrival." He waved a hand at her designer wedding dress.

"But I thought you asked Charlie's permission."

He looked away. "Ah, I sorta, ah, didn't."

"Holy moly, Rico." She yanked the earrings from her lobes as if they were on fire. Hurriedly, she wiped them on his sleeve. "Fingerprints," she muttered. "Hold out your hands." When he obeyed, she dropped them in his palms like they were hot potatoes. "Run, Rico!" She shoved him toward the door.

"I was just trying to help-" he cried, gone in a flash.

Francie sank down in a heap. The beautiful satin and lace material crumpled around her ankles and billowed up to her waist. The corset-like top dug into her ribs.

She groaned, dropping her head into her hands. "Please, let him put them back on time."

Her mind swirled with the punishment if he didn't. Not only would he suffer the consequences, but, no doubt everyone would discover she was in on it, too. Rico would not take it lightly and would ultimately blab the truth about her involvement.

It would be one more thing the employees would hate her for and maybe even try to get rid of her and her pesky, inexperienced sister, Priscilla. She'd had a feeling they were just looking for an opportunity to show them in a bad light and toss them out the door.

She cringed inwardly at the knowledge that her sister and she probably deserved it, too. With no skills to speak of, they'd bumbled through more than one chance and brought more ire their way. Charlie had kept them on, comforting the other employees. King's would give them a chance, just like King's had given every hard working employee an opportunity to prove themselves. How many more chances could she get, though?

With a huge sigh, Francie forced herself up to her feet and back into the dressing room. The first tug on the binds that squished her together didn't budge. "Huh?" She tried to snake one arm around her back and skimmed the tail end of the bow. 'Why did he tie it like this?" Reaching over her back with the other hand, she attempted to grab the ties that way. Her fingers missed, not able to latch on. She wrestled with it for some time, turning and twisting, even rubbing her back against the wall to try to dislodge the knot.

Beads of sweat clung to her forehead. She dashed those away only to have more form as she contorted again. "Rico, what in the world did you do to me?" she asked between gritted teeth.

Finally, with her arms aching from the effort, she gave up. She needed help. Now she longed for the cell phone she couldn't afford.

"I can do this," she whispered her new mantra again.

Blowing out a breath and a strand of hair out of her vision, she set her jaw and lifted her chin, slowly exiting the dressing area. "Please let me find Rico before anyone else finds me."

\*\*\*

Marcus Goode strode across the marble floor of King's Department Store. Stillness surrounded him. Looking up, he spotted a familiar face. "Bruno, my man, how have you been doing?"

He grasped the security guard's hand and they clapped each other on the back.

"Mr. Marcus, you're a sight for sore eyes. What's it been? Ten years?"

"Maybe more. I thought you'd be long gone by now."

"Me? Hah, I love this place. Come on, Miss Charlie's waiting for you."

Bruno punched in the code for the executive elevator and ushered Marcus in when it arrived.

"Not coming up?"

"Nah, got rounds to do. Make sure no one's lurking about. Then we can shut this baby up tight for the night."

"Fifth floor, right?"

"Yes, sir, never changed that, but there's been a whole lot of changes in the last few weeks. I hear you're going to be another one."

"*Temporary* change." Marcus emphasized the first word.

"That's what they all say." Before the doors closed, Bruno said, "Now Marcus B. Goode, you hear?"

Marcus chuckled at the old joke. Alone now in the enclosed muted gold compartment, he shook his head. His mother had named him Marcus B. Goode as a lifelong reminder to be good. Most people never knew his middle name was just an initial. Luckily, he'd never had to cope with their reactions when they found out. But some of his old childhood friends, including Bruno, always knew and ribbed him about it.

It reminded him of how much he missed the people in his life. Just like when he saw his mother earlier today at the nursing facility. When had she gotten so old and so weak? Was it just since she'd broken her hip and been in rehabilitation to mend it?

Years ago, he'd struck out in business on his own. His mother had several husbands along the way and, for the most part, she'd been happy. But after each divorce, Marcus would return to clean up any messes, make certain she had a nice place to live, support her, and did what any only son would do and take care of her. After all, it was his duty.

He'd promised his late father. And he never broke his promise.

Even if that meant keeping secrets from his mother to protect her.

The doors dinged open and he came back to the present.

A tall, model thin lady with a wide smile greeted him. In one arm, she cradled a clipboard. She stuck out her hand. "I'm Peg Newbury, your assistant."

He returned the surprisingly firm handshake. "Peg, nice to meet you. I'm Marcus."

"I know."

That made him chuckle. She joined him. "Come on, Superstar, Charlie's just finishing up and will meet us in your new office."

"Temporary office," he corrected.

Walking beside him down the corridor lined with conference rooms and offices, she leaned over and whispered, "Word is all this may be temporary if we don't get our stuff together in the next few weeks. Sales are up now, but will they remain up now that Charlie's easing back on her schedule because she's expecting?"

"That's why she called," he murmured in agreement.

"Who better to yank us back into the stratosphere than Marcus Goode, well respected, world renown businessman who built an empire from one restaurant in little ol' Dallas, Texas to dozens of restaurants and exclusive resorts in dozens of the most beautiful places on earth?"

"Put like that, I shouldn't have any problems, right?"

She winked at him. "None at all."

Grinning, he noted that Peg would be a welcome respite to the buttoned up businessmen he'd dealt with on a daily basis.

When they entered his new office with the black furniture and glass top desk, he stilled just inside the doorway. The enormity of what he was doing hit him then. He, Marcus Goode, would run King's Department Store for the next twelve weeks to honor the late, great Charles King, the man who took him under his wing when he was just a boy and his mother worked as a saleswoman. He would repay the King family for all they had done for his family.

"Marcus," Charlie cried out.

He turned just in time to see her rush to him and throw her arms around him. Hugging her back, he said, "It's been too long, my friend."

Pulling away, she said, "I've missed you, too. It's no fun getting into trouble here without you beside me."

Chuckling, he nodded. "Ah, the good old days."

"The dirt some people still have on us."

He recalled how years ago as kids they would poke their noses into every department, every little cubbyhole, and every nook and cranny. The things they used to see and hear astounded him to this day. "And we have on them," he said quietly, maybe too quietly.

Her smile faded. She remembered.

He could never forget that day.

All of a sudden his father had taken to picking up his mother from work. Only this day, he'd arrived early and hadn't told anyone. Marcus and Charlie were playing in the corner of the storage room, killing time when a noise yanked them from their game of hide and seek. He looked up and discovered his father kissing another woman. Shock rooted his feet to the spot. But the loving words the woman and the man he'd respected all his life exchanged crashed over him as if he'd been struck by a bolt of lightning.

Love? Forever? But he was supposed to love Marcus' mom for the rest of his life.

In the back of his mind, Marcus recalled the woman worked in the same department as his mother did.

That's when he felt his friend grab his arm and squeeze tight. He looked at Charlie's little face and saw the tear fall from the corner of her eye. He turned away from her hurt because he couldn't even face his own at the time.

They sat huddled there long after the grownups had left.

"I'm sorry," she whispered.

"Not as much as I am." His heart was breaking.

She swallowed hard. "I'll never tell."

He nodded, knowing she wouldn't either. "Thanks."

He came back to the moment with a crash. She never did tell. And for that he was eternally grateful. It was part of the reason he agreed to temporarily take over King's for her until she could find a permanent replacement. Lifelong friends who had each other's back did things like that for each other.

"I'll never be able to thank you enough for stepping in like this. You were the only one I trusted."

"I'm glad I could help." He'd rearranged a great deal, essentially handing over his business to his capable team, to be with his mom during her convalescence. He'd have had nothing to do for all these weeks if Charlie hadn't called. "It's not like I could just sit and twiddle my thumbs while mom's going through rehabilitation."

"How's your mom? I spoke to her a few days ago, but I don't think she understood everything I said."

"She has her good moments. She's getting better." Deep inside, he knew she struggled, not because of her hip, but because another man had broken her heart. Her boyfriend had dumped her just a day before she fell. Somehow she'd been so distracted over losing him that she hadn't paid attention to the step down and she'd landed heavily on her right hip.

But the physical pain was less taxing to her than her heartache. The depression was far worse. His mother was in love with love.

He'd tried for years to cure her of it; however he'd failed miserably.

But he'd held fast in his own life. He'd have nothing to do with love. It was a curse.

"Look, Marcus, it's great to see you and I wanted to fill you in before the manager's meeting tomorrow morning. But I'm expecting an important phone call and can't miss it. So why don't you explore the store and see all the changes. I'll catch up with you after my call and we can go over some things. How's that sound?"

"Great," he said with as much enthusiasm as he could muster. Maybe being here and reliving the past wasn't such a good idea after all. He'd made it a point to never look back and now he was being forced to face the demons of his past.

Raking up the ashes would only get him burnt again. He was already feeling the heat. How much more could he take?

# CHAPTER 2

Francie stuck her head out of the wedding department. The dim lights in the store didn't reveal anyone.

"Coast is clear," she whispered. Carefully, she made her way through each department. "Rico, where are you?" she asked in a low voice. No response.

Her heart sank at the thought of having to go downstairs to the jewelry department. Someone was sure to see her in the big, white wedding dress. It wasn't something she could easily explain away. Not this time.

Her body ached from carrying the heavy, crystal embossed one-of-a-kind designer gown. "It weighs a ton," she muttered, now realizing why brides often selected another dress to dance in at the reception.

"Note to self, when selecting your wedding dress consider the weight of it when trying to dance at your reception." Under her breath, she muttered, "At least I didn't try on the shoes yet." The three inch sparkly ones were still nestled in their box in the dressing room. "With my clothes. Ugh!"

Growing weary, Francie turned a corner and found herself in the linen department. The demo bed, piled with an assortment of pillows and the matching plush lilac duvet, looked enticing.

"I'll just sit for a minute. Get my breath back. Find my bearings. Make a plan." As she sank down, a sigh escaped her lips.

She hadn't realized how tired she was. She'd been up since six in the morning and it was after nine at night. Her long double shifts were getting the best of her. If only Priscilla would come to work instead of go out and play, she thought, then she could cut back on some hours. But someone needed to pay the bills.

Another sigh escaped. Her feet throbbed. Gingerly, she shifted her position and swung her feet up to rest on the bed. "Think," she begged her foggy brain. "How can I get out of this dress and stay out of hot water?"

The pillows were right there. She eased her head onto one. "Ah, nice, soft," she murmured. The knotted stays stuck into her spine. She turned on her left side, slipping her clasped hands under her cheek.

In the back of her mind, Francie knew Rico wasn't coming back for her. Had she even told him to? She didn't remember now. Her concern focused on getting the earrings back in the vault without anyone discovering they'd been missing in the first place.

As her mind continued to whirl with thoughts, her tired body relaxed into the lush softness surrounding her. "Just another minute and I'll get up," she promised herself.

How would she get out of the expensive dress without damaging it or letting anyone else know? Maybe she could sleep there all night long and wait for Charlie. Her stepsister came in before seven. After all, the bed was much more comfortable then the couch she'd been sleeping on the last few weeks.

Then a disturbing thought rushed through her busy mind. There's a new temporary man taking over tomorrow. Would her stepsister be so involved with meetings with him that she wouldn't walk the floor before the store opened as she usually did?

Francie could go to the guard station and get help. But they would tell.

Her cheeks grew warm. The things they'd say about her then. Everyone would know her secret. She'd never be able to sneak into the wedding dress department and try on the new arrivals again.

How could she ever find the perfect wedding dress then?

\*\*\*

Marcus quietly walked through each department, noting the dramatic changes on the first floor and seeing the much needed updates on the second. He lingered in the housewares department. The shiny, copper-bottomed pots and pans caused him to smile as he recalled his early restaurant days, loving how he could create something out of a few ingredients.

One thing he'd gotten from his mother was her love of cooking. He picked up fast at her elbow and cooked her full meals by the age of seven. His father, a traveling salesman, was on the road so often it seemed like it was always Marcus and his mother while he grew up.

At the thought of his now deceased father and his betrayal, Marcus frowned and turned away from the housewares.

But it nagged at him, how his father scoffed at his interest in cooking. Marcus played in every sport imaginable and loved the competition. He loved football the most. But, after blowing out his knee in college, Marcus had to find a career he was just as passionate about. The restaurant business was the perfect fit for him. He could cook, use his people and business skills, and make money at the same time.

And he did. The long hours he dedicated to his business brought him more recognition than he'd ever considered. He branched out to being a guest chef, with no formal training, to hotels, then resorts. He'd find little gems, risk buying them, redo each one from top to bottom, and make them sparkle even more. It worked.

He smiled. Pride surged through him. He loved the process of taking something and building it up to its potential. Most times, even going beyond its potential.

Now he focused on the store. He'd done it before. He could do it here.

With more confidence then he'd felt since agreeing to the temporary position, Marcus strode down the wide store aisles. In his mind, he made mental notes on the changes he thought would bring King's back into the limelight.

Going by the linens, he glanced at the displays. His eyes caught something odd. Turning back sharply, he stopped at the bed. "I'm seeing things," he murmured. Blinking a few times, he realized the image stayed the same.

The woman slept soundly. He took in every detail of her from her honey blonde hair to her bare shoulders onto the swell of her cleavage. The expensive wedding dress clung to her small waist and the slight curve of her hip. Her bare toes, the nails painted a delicate pink, peeked out from the bottom folds of fluffy fabric at the hem.

Marcus drew nearer. She was even more beautiful up close. The pale pink flush sweeping cheeks and her perfect bow lips caused his heart to beat a little quicker. He swallowed hard.

She was saying something in her sleep. He couldn't hear. Bending down on one knee beside her, he couldn't stop himself from reaching out and brushing the soft blonde tendrils off of her cheek.

"Tickles." She giggled.

He chuckled, fascinated by this lovely creature.

Her perfume rose to him, subtle, yet alluring. He breathed in deeply. Heat rushed through his body.

Her rose colored lips curved into a gentle smile. He focused on them, the full bottom one and the perfectly shaped bow of the top one. "What would it feel like to kiss you?" he whispered.

She mumbled something. He dipped his head closer to understand. "How do I get out of this dress?"

Marcus laughed. "I'll help," he offered as he leaned in to touch his lips against hers…

**Waking Sleeping Beauty is available now.**

# ABOUT THE AUTHOR

Laurie LeClair writes contemporary romance and women's fiction. Laurie's habit of daydreaming has gotten her into a few scrapes and launched her to take up her dream of writing. Finally, she can put all those stories in her head to rest as she brings them to life on the page. Laurie considers herself a New Texan (New England born and raised and now living in Texas). She lives in Central Texas with her husband Jim. She loves to hear from her readers.

**You can contact Laurie at:**
https://twitter.com/LeClairbooks
https://facebook.com/laurieleclair.75

## Other books by Laurie LeClair
Once Upon A Romance Series:
If The Shoes Fits – Book 1
Waking Sleeping Beauty – Book 2
Taming McGruff – Book 3

Made in United States
Orlando, FL
06 February 2024

43362573R00134